I0573586

FRANKLIN VERSUS THE SOUL THIEF

THE CHRONICLES OF FRANKLIN: BOOK TWO

LEAH R CUTTER

KNOTTED ROAD PRESS

Franklin Versus The Soul Thief
The Chronicles of Franklin: Book Two
Copyright © 2015 Leah Cutter
All rights reserved
Published by Knotted Road Press
www.KnottedRoadPress.com

ISBN: 978-1-64470-003-7

Cover Art:
ID 41487519 © Vasilev | Dreamstime.com
ID 14457747 © Gan Hui | Dreamstime.com
ID 30569429 © Camrocker | Dreamstime.com

Cover and interior design copyright © 2015 Knotted Road Press
http://www.KnottedRoadPress.com

Come someplace new…
If you'd like to be notified of new releases, sign up for my newsletter.

I will never spam you or use your email for nefarious purposes. You can also unsubscribe at any time.

http://www.LeahCutter.com/newsletter/

The Cassie Stories

Poisoned Pearls

Tainted Waters

Spoiled Harvest

Bloodied Ice

Contemporary Fantasy

Siren's Call

The Immortals' War

Circle of Air

CHAPTER 1

FRANKLIN SAT OUTSIDE in his backyard, watching the knee-high cornstalks grow. A ghost sat beside him, on the other white-metal garden chair. Franklin didn't know the ghost's name—he'd never pushed one toward Franklin. The ghost's *intent* had been difficult to read as well.

But the ghost had joined Franklin every morning for the last week, the pair of them sitting on either side of the white metal garden table, listening to the morning birds and the quiet hum of the interstate as the dew evaporated and the day began. The Kentucky blue-grass Franklin grew back there was still so new, the spring color so bright, it was likely to hurt your eyes.

The ghost was a white man. He wore what he'd been buried in, like all ghosts—a light blue suit with a dark blue tie and a white shirt, probably his Sunday best.

A black man, like Franklin, probably would have worn something a little more somber. Plus, Franklin had always planned on being buried in a hat. It would just be more formal if he was wearing a hat. He'd bought a black Stetson for the occasion, though he'd never told no one about it, not even Mama, either when she'd been alive or when she'd come back to haunt Franklin as a ghost.

Not that Franklin planned on dying anytime soon. He was still a young man, not yet even thirty. He still had a lot of living to do yet.

But this ghost, this white man...Franklin had the impression that he hadn't lived a lot while he'd been, well, with the living. Even if there was a Heaven beyond where they was sitting, Franklin guessed the ghost was afraid to take those final steps.

Franklin always reckoned that dying was hard on a body, not just 'cause they were passing out of this earth. Ghosts couldn't make any noise, not generally, and they was rarely strong enough to lift even a single piece of paper.

So every morning, Franklin tried to encourage his guest. He didn't want the ghost not to feel welcome. Mama had taught him better than that. However, the ghost needed to move on. It was part of the natural course of things.

"Now, I know it might be scary," Franklin told the ghost as he sipped his sweet tea. He'd added a sprig of mint to it that morning, so it tasted cool and fresh. "But it's still the next step. The right thing to do."

Franklin always tried to do the right thing and to do his duty. Mama had insisted that meant helping the dead pass on, out of this life and into the next. Franklin weren't perfect. No man was. Still, he tried.

The ghost just shook his head, looking down at his hands, tightly clenched.

Normally, when a ghost had trouble passing from this world to the next, it was because they still had some deed left undone. Like the older woman Franklin had helped the week before last. She'd been a black woman, ponderous and ample-bosomed, wearing the brightest red dress that Franklin had ever seen on a ghost. She couldn't leave, not until she'd seen her boy one last time.

Though she'd been as big as Mama, she'd ridden as daintily as a little girl between the handlebars of Franklin's bike as he drove her into Katherinesville, then beyond, to the graveyard. Then he'd waited with her until her son had arrived.

"Now, I know new things can be frightening," Franklin consoled the ghost sitting beside him in his backyard. "Hell, I remember the

2

first time I really kissed a girl. Felt like my heart was about to pound outa my chest." He paused, relishing the memory of his first kisses with Julie, how shy he'd been, how wonderful it had all turned out. "I figure this is that same level of scared for you. But you gonna have to try."

The man nodded.

Franklin knew the ghost needed something. He just weren't sure what.

"I believe you didn't try a lot of new things when you was living," Franklin said delicately.

The ghost's head dropped down, his hands clenched even tighter. If he weren't already so pale, Franklin would bet they turned even whiter.

"But this here's a *new* new thing. Something that you're only going to get to try once. Not just have to try. But *get* to try. Most folks just go along into Heaven, lifted up and not making a choice or a decision about it all. You, on the other hand, get to walk there all on your lonesome."

The man went from staring at his hands to looking pensively out at Franklin's field.

Was there a gate to Heaven there, among the rows of corn? Franklin had always found it a calming place, with just blue sky above him and the smell of rich dirt and growing things surrounding him.

"You should try it," Franklin urged.

The man glanced back at Franklin, then finally, decisively, stood up. He nodded once at Franklin, nodded his thanks, then strode off purposefully into the cornfield. He faded as he walked, as if stepping into a mist Franklin couldn't see.

Franklin took a deep breath, feeling the satisfaction of a job well done. That ghost had finally moved on.

Maybe he wasn't going to Heaven. Maybe there was another, in-between place, that he'd visit first. Franklin didn't rightly know.

However, he never felt fear from any ghost about passing on, so he always figured it were Heaven or some equivalent. That he weren't encouraging folk to pass into Hell. He hoped so.

Franklin leaned back in his chair and took another sip of his sweet tea, mint fresh and cool. Even Mama might say he'd done good. That he done his duty, his job.

Crap.

Helping ghosts pass wasn't Franklin's only job. It might take all his time if he'd let it, however, it sure didn't pay the bills.

And he was gonna be late again.

Luckily, Karl would understand.

Sort of.

Franklin hurried back to the house, pausing and blinking when he stepped inside, trying to get his eyes to adjust to the dim light. Though it was still spring, the sun was starting to find its heat, and he'd left the shades down to give the house a fighting chance against it.

The farm report still murmured in the background from the ancient TV sitting on an equally ancient bureau in the living room. Franklin hurriedly turned it off, noting that no rain was predicted, which wasn't all that unusual.

It might mean a dry summer, though. That wouldn't be great for his crops. He'd have to keep an eye on the forecast.

He passed through the living room into the dining room, the long table pressed up against the southern wall with all the windows. He was going to have to invite his cousins over for Sunday dinner again, sometime soon. They generally gathered every week at Aunt Jasmine's place, after church, but Franklin had had them over once, and so had his cousin May, trading Sundays with Aunt Jasmine. He'd like to do that again.

Franklin hadn't invited Julie to Sunday dinner over at Aunt Jasmine's or at May's, though he'd thought about it. But he would invite her the next time they had dinner at his house, regardless of how mercilessly his cousins teased him afterward about his white girlfriend.

In the kitchen, the light over the stove was still on. Franklin never turned it off. For more than a year after her death, Mama had haunted Franklin, mostly sticking to the kitchen, sitting at the table there. As a ghost, she'd always cast enough light for him to see.

The light above the stove wasn't the same. It was still better than nothing.

Franklin hurriedly rinsed out his glass and set it on the rack with the dishes from breakfast. He nearly called out that he'd be back later that night, but there was no one to tell his plans to.

Not since Mama had passed, no longer worried about her boy.

Franklin still checked the gears on his bike, along with the chain, before he hopped on. He'd never had a vengeful ghost, and most ghosts didn't have the power to break stuff. Still, it didn't hurt to check. Every time.

Finally, Franklin pedaled up his gravel driveway and onto the paved lane. Though Franklin could drive a car (and he renewed his driver's license faithfully) he didn't own one. He didn't like to take chances like that. If a ghost suddenly popped up while he was riding, he could just fall off his bike. If he was driving a car, he might hurt someone.

Before Franklin reached the end of the lane, the phone in his pocket chirped. Though Franklin was already late, he still stopped and flipped it open.

It was Julie. A text with just the word "Morning!" followed by a smiley face.

Franklin stopped, smiling himself. He didn't have a smart phone —as Mama had said, those things made you stupid—so it weren't easy for him to text back. Julie understood that, though. He'd send her back a note sometime later, when he had time to carefully spell out all the words.

It was odd, being so connected to someone. His cousin Darryl had teased Franklin about being tied on an electronic leash, but it didn't feel that way to Franklin. Instead, it was just a way to share his day with Julie.

Franklin started back down the lane. At the end of it, he turned onto Steven's Road. It was a much busier street, with cars whizzing by. Franklin always drove along the gravel at the side of the road so he wouldn't be hit.

It was about two miles along Steven's Road to the big highway. It was actually safer for him to ride along the highway, as it was a four-lane road with wide, paved shoulders that Franklin could ride on.

He didn't have to ride far along the highway anymore. He no longer worked at the grocery store in town. Instead, Franklin now worked with his greatest competitor, Karl, at Karl's farm-fresh vegetable stand.

Franklin hadn't been able to compete with Karl the previous year for the Kentucky State Fair blue ribbon for who grew the best popping corn—his field had been destroyed by an evil creature, with him and Karl fighting it.

This year, however, would be different. Franklin had his first crop in already, and was determined as ever to win.

"'Bout time you showed up," Karl drawled as Franklin parked his bike behind the fruit and vegetable stand. The stand was about three car-lengths long, and about the width of Karl's pickup. It was a solid building, not just a flimsy shack, with power for the two large fridges in the back and fans constantly blowing, along with a watering system for the vegetables.

The front had slanted wooden racks, where the produce was stacked. They were long enough that Franklin—who was close to six feet tall—had to stand on his tiptoes to reach the bottom of them from the inside.

There were four people waiting to be served. Franklin recognized a couple of them—like Jesse, the chef, who claimed they sold the best greens in all of Wesley County.

"Sorry," Franklin told Karl.

Karl just frowned at him, his blue eyes glaring out from under his bushy brown eyebrows. He had a pointed nose and a sharp chin, made more pointed by his neatly trimmed goatee and mustache. He wore a tight black T-shirt and jeans that showed just how wiry and muscular he was.

Franklin was just as muscular, but he had more flesh on him. They were matched in height and weight, though.

Franklin had teased Karl more than once that he looked the perfect image of a good ole boy, looking like one of those Civil War generals in the old-timey photographs.

Fortunately for Franklin, Karl was a lot more than just that.

Franklin helped the next customer in line, weighing his bag of lettuce before explaining to Karl. "Had a guest."

It was the shorthand they'd come up with to talk about Franklin's *other* duties.

"I figured," Karl said sourly. "The guy in the suit? The one you was telling me about?"

Franklin nodded, giving Karl a wide grin. "Finally left."

And that was the last Franklin thought about that ghost for the rest of the day.

ONCE THE MORNING rush of folks buying vegetables and fruit petered off, Karl went to go tend his fields, leaving Franklin in charge of the stand. They'd worked out a good rhythm between them, Franklin coming in later most mornings as he dealt with the ghosts, Karl then leaving to finish off his chores and meet with suppliers. He'd come back and spell Franklin for a while in the afternoon, then they'd both have to be there during the "dinner rush"—people buying produce to have with their meal that night.

Sometimes ghosts followed Franklin to the stand and stayed with him for most of the day. He'd only had the one angry ghost since he'd started working there eight months before. The ghost had knocked over more than one of the careful piles of apples, trying to get Franklin to leave and take him up to Wolf River.

Most of the ghosts was just lost souls, though, and merely watched the living with sad eyes.

Franklin saw more ghosts these days than he used to. He didn't know if it was because he'd gotten some kind of reputation in the ghost community, or if he'd gotten more powerful since he'd fought that creature in his cornfield the year before. Maybe it was a bit of both.

Today, though, no one was bothering him, either customers or ghosts. Franklin was able to turn his attention to his one true love —popcorn.

At the back of the stand, but still close enough that Franklin could see anyone walking up, he'd set up a propane tank with a single burner. He also had one of those hand-crank stovetop popcorn makers.

Franklin was experimenting with a blend of corn that day. He kept the different varieties of kernels sealed in white porcelain jars that he'd got from the Goodwill, meant for fancy coffee beans.

While Franklin only grew yellow, Grade A American popping corn in his field, that didn't mean he didn't branch out and experiment now and again, tasting different types of popping corn.

They sold popcorn at the stand in the afternoons, generally to the kids who would stop by on their way home from school.

Franklin only wanted to charge a nickel a bag, and when Karl wasn't looking, he sometimes did. But only when the youngsters was respectful, calling him "Mr. Kanly" and remembering their P's and Q's. The rest of the time it was a quarter a bag. A bargain for some of the best tasting popcorn Franklin could cook up.

Today, Franklin was working with a mixture of fine yellow corn that had really nice wings on it when it popped with a strawberry corn that had a sweetness to it as well as a solid crunch. It was difficult to cook them together, as the two different types of kernels tended to pop at different times, with different temperatures.

Franklin had just about got the timing perfect, though. He started with the freshest lard, melting it in the pan, then swirling it just right, coating the bottom of the pan as well as a bit up the sides. Then he added the strawberry corn. Those hard kernels needed more time, more coaxing, to produce the perfect popping corn.

When the strawberry corn was sizzling just right, Franklin added the yellow corn. He gently shook the pan in a circle, getting all the kernels coated evenly with the melted lard.

As the first kernels started popping, Franklin started stirring the pot with the built-in crank.

"Hey, anyone here?"

Franklin jumped, startled. He'd been so busy with his popping corn he hadn't heard anyone drive up.

Fortunately, it was just Sheriff Thompson. "Be right there!" Franklin called to him.

The sheriff nodded. "Take your time." He stood and ran his thumb and forefinger across and then down his brown mustache, the only thing that was soft about his face. He had a big nose and hard brown eyes, a chiseled chin and thin lips that was generally pushed together in a line of disapproval.

Sheriff Thompson hadn't been giving Franklin as hard of a time lately. Especially since Franklin had stayed out of trouble for the last nine months or so.

"Smells good," the sheriff called as Franklin finished up, the popping corn bubbling up and out of the pan.

"New blend," Franklin told him. He finished popping the corn— only a few unpopped kernels remained at the bottom of the pan. After he poured the freshly popped corn into a bowl, he added a drizzle of warm lard and a sprinkle of salt. He carried the bowl with him as he approached the front of the stand.

"What can I do for you?" Franklin asked the sheriff. He handed the bowl across the stand so the sheriff could try it.

Sheriff plucked a few kernels out of the bowl, then tossed them into his mouth.

"That's good," he said. He seemed surprised. He tried a few more kernels, picking them up delicately instead of grabbing a handful.

"Can get you a bag to go," Franklin offered. He didn't figure Karl would mind him giving away free popping corn to the sheriff. Not as a bribe, not exactly. But just so the sheriff wouldn't decide to give them a hard time later on.

"Naw," Sheriff Thompson said, though he took three more kernels. "I'll be spending the rest of the afternoon picking hulls out from my teeth."

"I understand," Franklin said, though he'd never had that problem. His teeth were strong and he'd never had a cavity.

"You see much traffic out here?" the sheriff asked, casually looking around.

Franklin didn't believe that the sheriff really did *casual*. He was looking for something.

"We get some," Franklin said, shrugging. The sheriff had come to their stand a couple times when he'd been off duty, coming with his wife, buying a basket of apples once last fall, and the first of the imported strawberries, earlier that spring.

When the sheriff didn't continue, Franklin asked, "Is there someone in particular you're looking for?"

The sheriff turned his disapproving gaze at Franklin. "No. I'm not looking for someone. I'm just wondering…"

Franklin stood patiently while the sheriff looked off again. "We do see a lot of customers on the weekends," Franklin finally volunteered.

"Good." Sheriff Thompson turned and fixed his hard stare at Franklin. "We got this charity ball coming up. I was figuring maybe we could put up some posters. Sell some tickets."

Though Franklin, technically, owned half of Karl's vegetable stand —they'd formed an LLC and he had the paperwork to prove it and everything—Franklin still shook his head and scratched at the back of his neck.

"I don't know," he said. "I'd have to check with the boss."

"The boss, huh," Sheriff Thompson said. "You want me to believe you just work here?"

Franklin gave the sheriff a sheepish grin. "I do work here. Every day. Except Sundays. Got church, then."

The sheriff nodded. "You've kept your nose clean. I'll give you that. Still don't like what happened last year."

Franklin shrugged. There weren't nothing he could do about the past.

"Tell you what. You buy a couple of tickets and I'll stop bugging you," Sheriff Thompson said. "You could take that girl of yours to it. Have a real nice night out."

"Whatchyou say it was again?" Franklin asked.

"Kentucky law enforcement memorial charity ball. With a silent auction." The sheriff handed over two tickets.

Franklin gave a low whistle. The amount per ticket was more than he made in a week.

Of course, he had a good bit of money saved up. He tried to live cheaply, looking to buy the property next to his so he could expand his fields. Mrs. Averson still wouldn't bring down the price, though the fields there had been standing fallow for years.

"I'm not sure about buying any tickets," Franklin said slowly.

"It's for charity," the sheriff pointed out. "You'll get a nice meal and wine and everything."

Franklin didn't drink much, and certainly not wine.

"When's your girl's birthday?" Sheriff Thompson asked.

Franklin thought. They'd celebrated her birthday in November. He was glad he had dark skin, so the sheriff couldn't see him blush at the memory of that night.

Would she like going out someplace fancy like this? Probably not. She weren't no more fancy than Franklin was.

"I'll ask her," Franklin said, pushing the tickets back at the sheriff.

Sheriff Thompson put the tickets back inside his jacket pocket. He looked up and down the stand sourly.

Franklin braced himself.

"You know, y'all need to be careful on the weekends when you got more customers coming and going. Could be a hazard to traffic on the highway."

"I'll make sure Karl knows," Franklin replied, keeping his tone light.

The sheriff wouldn't really shut them down that weekend, would he? If they didn't agree to sell his tickets?

Franklin wasn't sure what he should do, but he didn't like being bullied. "Y'all have a good day now," he called out after the sheriff as he got in his brown Crown Vic and left.

Maybe Karl would have an idea about what to do. Or maybe Franklin should have agreed to put up some posters. He sure didn't want to try to keep track of some kind of charity ball tickets while he was trying to help customers as well. It'd be too easy for some of them to get lost, and he'd end up being responsible.

And Franklin just couldn't afford that.

FRANKLIN PEDALED HOME LATE that night. Karl and Franklin had talked long after they'd closed the stand about the sheriff. They'd decided that the next time the sheriff came by, they'd offer him a table out front, so he or his deputies could sell tickets to the charity ball.

Neither of them wanted to be responsible for selling tickets. Not that the sheriff was crooked, but he still might accuse them of not working hard enough, not selling enough tickets for him.

As Franklin rolled his bike down his driveway, the spirit of Sweet Bess appeared. Sweet Bess had been a hog Franklin had slaughtered over a year ago. She'd been a mean critter when she'd been alive, and a killer. More than one small bird and ground squirrel had found that out.

But it had made her meat extra sweet. Franklin still remembered the lard he'd rendered from her. He'd been careful using it, making it last as long as he could.

What did Sweet Bess want with him now? The last time she'd appeared like this in his driveway had been to warn him of the creature lying in wait for him inside his house.

Sweet Bess stared at Franklin from the side yard. Stared hard at him.

Then she turned and ambled back that way.

Did she expect him to follow her?

Franklin set his bike in the shed and walked around the side of his house. The evening had already settled in, cool and clean. No rain still and the air felt dry. The crickets and cicadas hadn't reached their full summer chorus strength, when they'd be deafening. No, it was still a peaceful racket, joined by the frogs in the pond that sat in the middle of Mrs. Averson's fields, that would turn to cracked dirt when the heat of summer started cooking everything.

A ghost sat on one of Franklin's white metal chairs in the backyard.

Why would Sweet Bess want Franklin to come and greet this ghost? It weren't like there weren't plenty of ghosts passing through all the time.

It was a white man, who had a soft glow to him, like all ghosts did, particularly at night. He was wearing a light blue suit.

Normally, Franklin didn't like coming out into his backyard in the evenings. The fields seemed to give the ghosts extra power, making him uncomfortable when they pushed their *intent* at him.

"Howdy," Franklin said, greeting the ghost.

The ghost looked at him and rose slowly from his seat.

Franklin stopped, puzzled. That sure looked like the guy he'd helped pass that morning. In fact, as the ghost drew closer to Franklin, he was positive of it.

"What happened?" Franklin asked. It didn't make no sense. Once a ghost passed, they was gone. They never came back.

The man's eyes had changed. Instead of looking faded and a little lost, now they looked black and hollow.

Then he opened his mouth and howled.

The sound made Franklin shiver all the way to his core.

How had the ghost done that? It weren't a loud howl. It was knife-thin and eerie, floating across the open yard.

But Franklin heard it. That scream. That awful cry of pain.

"What the hell happened to you?" Franklin asked.

Whatever it was, it weren't good.

CHAPTER 2

Franklin shivered inside his house, sitting alone at his kitchen table, listening to the ghost howling in his backyard. He'd had a light supper, burgers fried in bacon fat with thick cheese and ketchup, along with the first of the tomatoes and the last of the sweet onions. And because Julie had been bugging him about eating more vegetables, he'd also fried up some green peppers to go with them.

He'd been barely able to eat, however, with that ghost making that racket. Now he sat drinking a beer, the house dim.

He sure hoped Mrs. Averson next door couldn't hear the ghost. It wouldn't do to disturb his neighbors that way. Didn't matter none that he weren't the one making the noise.

There was that empty field between his place and her house, but the howls the ghost made carried and cut through to the soul.

At least the howling ghost had stayed outside. What would happen if he decided to come inside?

Franklin didn't know what to do. He'd done his duty. He'd helped that ghost pass.

Had this been why the ghost hadn't wanted to go? Had he known that he'd get…thrown back? Franklin didn't know. But that kind of made sense.

Except he would have thought the ghost would have been more scared the first time, if he'd known this was coming.

And what kind of ghost made noises like that? Franklin had *never* met a ghost who howled like this. He'd been helping ghosts pass since he was fourteen. He'd met all kinds. Nothing like this.

It sure looked like a ghost. Kind of felt like a ghost, though his eyes were more haunted.

What had happened to him?

Franklin didn't know what to do. If his cousin Lexine hadn't been killed by the creature the year before, he could have asked her, though she'd dealt more with spirits of animals and places, while he dealt with humans.

Who else could he ask? Who would know?

Franklin had never met anyone special like he was. His cousin Darryl had a different kind of special, one that involved being in the woods and hunting.

Maybe Eddie would know—the lady who was the head of the pagan group that his girlfriend Julie belonged to. Franklin had never gone back to that group, had always made excuses every time Julie had asked. It was just too hard to see Eddie. She'd refused her gifts, wouldn't move how the spirits wanted her to go.

Maybe she'd know something about an out-of-place ghost, however. He'd have to talk with Julie, maybe accept her next invitation to go visit the group.

Franklin finished his beer, then quickly drank down a second. He weren't much of a drinker, never had been. He hoped the alcohol would help him sleep through the howling.

Because he sure had no idea what else to do.

IN THE MORNING, the ghost was still there, though he'd grown quiet. Franklin went out to sit with him after breakfast, like he had for the week before that.

"Can you tell me what happened?" Franklin asked quietly. "Why you came back?"

The ghost stared intently out into Franklin's field, as if he was searching for that portal out of there again.

"I don't know how to help you," Franklin said.

The ghost finally looked at Franklin and nodded.

"What do you need?" Franklin asked. The first time he'd met this ghost, he'd never really pushed his *intent* toward Franklin.

Now, the ghost's eyes was too haunted. And lost. There wasn't anything the ghost knew. He didn't have something compelling to do. Or something equally compelling to keep him there.

He was just stuck.

"I'd help you if I could," Franklin told the man.

The ghost sighed, the sound carrying on the wind. He seemed more solid that morning as well, his light blue suit like a gash in the morning light instead of blending in.

He didn't belong there, back on earth, sitting in Franklin's backyard. That was what kept striking Franklin. That ghost just didn't fit.

Franklin didn't recall feeling that way about the other ghosts he'd helped. Dying was part of living. Sure, the ghosts needed to move on, but that, too, was part of the natural order of things.

There weren't nothing natural about this ghost—how he was stuck, what he needed to help him along. How lost his eyes looked.

Though the ghost didn't ask Franklin to stay, he sat for a while anyway, soaking in the calm morning air. Franklin didn't want to admit that maybe he didn't want to go to the stand, didn't want to have to deal with Sheriff Thompson.

He hadn't slept well that night either, not with all the howling.

Still, Franklin couldn't delay for too long.

Just like he had a duty to his ghosts, he also had a duty to Karl.

Besides, maybe that afternoon he could try a different combination of popping corn.

FRANKLIN GAVE a low whistle as he rode his bike up to the fruit and vegetable stand after his afternoon break. He'd gone back to his house, hoping that maybe the ghost had passed along, but had only gotten howled at for his questions.

Seemed as though Karl and the sheriff had come to some kind of agreement.

Posters for the charity ball were plastered on the sides of the shed, as well as across the front, obscuring Karl's name and the rest of the fancily painted sign. Hanging from the sign they had next to the highway was a large plaque, advertising the KYLEM Charity Auction and Ball.

A picture of a gold shield against a bright blue background took up most of the poster, with bold black letters proclaiming the event. Under that were all the particulars.

Franklin had to admit the posters were catchy. But did they really have to be up everywhere?

Karl just glared at Franklin as he came up, not even bothering to say hello. So Franklin just helped the next customer, not asking his partner any questions until the rush had died down for a bit and they'd finished restocking.

"What happened?" Franklin asked quietly.

Karl shook his head, crossed his arms over his chest and leaned back against a corner of the stand. "Sheriff came out. When I said we'd help, two deputies got out of his car and started putting up posters everywhere while the sheriff kept jabbering at me."

"It ain't right, covering up our stand that way," Franklin said.

"I know that," Karl replied, heatedly.

"It's our stand," Franklin said. "We get to say how many posters are put up."

"You gonna take them down?" Karl asked. He seemed surprised.

"Yup."

This felt too much like bullying, and Franklin flat-out *refused* to be bullied. Particularly by Sheriff Thompson.

Franklin walked out from the stand and into the cool evening air. He didn't want to take down all the posters—it was for charity, after all. But they didn't need to be everywhere.

He started at the side. He was tall enough to reach the ones up high, but as those didn't cover the fruit stand sign, he left them.

But he tore down a bunch more, until there was only three on that side.

When Franklin moved out to the front of the stand, Karl joined him.

"How about we take down the ones in the center, but leave the ones on either side?" Karl suggested.

"That's good. It'll look balanced," Franklin replied.

Karl helped Franklin take down some of the posters from the front of the stand, as well as some of the ones on the other side.

When Franklin stepped back, it looked like a normal fruit and vegetable stand again. Sure, some of the words painted on the stand were covered over. But enough letters were showing through that people could read the sign.

"What do you think the sheriff will say?" Karl asked.

"Don't care," Franklin said.

"You're a stubborn one, ain't you?" Karl said, shaking his head and giving Franklin a sly grin.

Franklin just shrugged. "It ain't about being stubborn. It's about being right."

And Franklin knew he was right about this. Just as he'd been right the year before, refusing to give the sheriff his fingerprints.

Of course, the sheriff had got his way anyway. Franklin's fingerprints were now in the system, though he'd tried so hard to stay on the right side of the law.

Maybe the sheriff would come back and complain. Or maybe he wouldn't notice. Franklin thought the posters looked better, now that there were fewer of them. It looked more professional, maybe.

Whatever the sheriff thought, Franklin was sure he'd find out about it in the morning.

FRANKLIN DIDN'T SLEEP WELL that night, not with the ghost howling again. What did it want? Why was it haunting him without telling him how to help him pass?

Was it really a ghost?

As Franklin was checking his bike that morning, making sure that nothing had happened to it, he felt a cold wind down his back.

That generally meant another ghost had shown up.

Franklin sighed. It was his duty, he knew. He'd wondered if the loud, howling ghost had scared off the others. Since the previous year, he'd generally had two or three ghosts visiting at the same time. It took some effort, trying to figure out what each one wanted. But it was his duty, and Franklin was usually happy to do it.

Franklin turned to see what new ghost had shown up. Karl would understand him being late. Again.

But it weren't a new ghost.

It was the lady Franklin had helped earlier that month, the ghost in the bright red dress, who he'd taken to the graveyard to talk with her son.

Franklin swallowed. Fear spiked through him. What was going on?

The woman's dark skin had grown darker, and her eyes were black holes. The red of her dress had darkened as well, looking less like happy poppies and more like blood.

She fixed him with a piercing stare then opened her mouth.

And howled.

～

FRANKLIN CAREFULLY COUNTED out the customer's change twice. He'd made a couple of mistakes earlier that morning. At least the folks had been honest about it, coming back and returning the extra change.

"What's going on with you?" Karl asked when the morning rush had cleared away. He had his usual dour expression on, though Franklin wondered if there was a hint of worry there as well.

"Too many ghosts," Franklin said cautiously. He weren't about to tell Karl his real problems. Hell, he weren't sure what his real problem was.

Were they ghosts? They didn't sound like ghosts. The guy in the backyard was getting more solid, too. Like he was starting to return to this world, having bounced out of the next.

Would he get strong enough to start tearing apart Franklin's fields?

And why had that woman reappeared? She'd done what she'd needed to do. She'd *passed*. Why had she come back? And what did she want now? Besides to howl at Franklin?

"Okay," Karl said, nodding. "You okay for staying here on your own this morning?"

"Yeah," Franklin said. He was tired, but he wouldn't fall asleep on the job. And besides, none of the ghosts had followed him to the stand.

"All right," Karl said. He pushed himself off the counter where he'd been leaning. "If the sheriff comes by, you don't let him give you any grief."

Franklin snorted. "Sure thing." He was so tired he might give the sheriff a piece of his mind if he showed up.

"Got any plans for tonight?" Karl asked as he made his way through the back of the stand and out toward his truck.

"Julie's coming over for dinner," Franklin said. He'd even put fresh sheets on the bed. Not that there was any guarantee they'd get to using them. Julie might be tired too. That had happened once or twice. Franklin was still hopeful, however.

Karl gave Franklin a grin. "Maybe I should come back early so you can nap. Save up your strength for later."

Franklin just rolled his eyes. "Yeah, yeah. Get going, so you can get back."

"Sure thing, lover boy," Karl teased.

Franklin just rolled his eyes again.

After Karl had gone, Franklin swept up the loose dirt on the inside of the stand. The floor was just rough boards laid down. If Franklin ever dropped anything, he had to be careful picking it back up, or he might get splinters. While he was breaking down the empty boxes he served a couple more customers, Mr. Hanson from just up the way and a tourist passing through.

Franklin was just about ready to start up the propane gas tank and try his hand at some more popping corn when the sheriff's brown Crown Vic pulled up.

Sheriff Thompson got out of his car and took a long look up and down the stand. Then he grinned at Franklin. "Looks mighty nice. Glad you boys agreed that this place needed some sprucing up."

Franklin opened his mouth to reply, then shut it again. Wouldn't do him no good, and he really didn't want to get on the bad side of the sheriff.

"You got deputies coming by tomorrow to sell tickets?" Franklin asked as the sheriff came up.

He nodded. "That I do. You sure you don't want a pair of tickets?"

"I'll be seeing Julie tonight. Will ask her," Franklin said. That way, it wasn't just him saying no.

Not that Franklin couldn't stand up to the sheriff if he set his mind to it. Mama might call him all kinds of fool for doing it, but Franklin didn't care.

It weren't right, the sheriff trying to bully them that way.

"Now, you sure you don't want to try and sell some of these tickets on your own?" the sheriff asked.

"No, sir," Franklin said. "Don't want to be responsible for them that way." Too easy for them to get lost or the money not accounted for or something.

"There's a prize for the officer who sells the most tickets," Sheriff Thompson admitted.

"What, you gonna split it with us?" Franklin asked.

The sheriff snorted. "Not likely."

Franklin shrugged. "No reason for us to sell any, then," he said.

The sheriff nodded. He leaned against the front of the stand, looked out at the semi passing by on the highway, then asked, "You been hearing any strange sounds out at your place lately?"

Damn it. Was the ghosts howling loud enough that the neighbors could hear?

"No, sir," Franklin lied. "What kind of sounds?" He made himself take deep breaths and stay loose and calm, just like they did on TV.

The sheriff turned to stare at Franklin with his hard, beady eyes.

"I think you're lying. There's been complaints of eerie sounds coming from your place. I think that some kind of trouble's starting up again. And I don't want any part of it. You hear me?"

Franklin gave the sheriff an easy nod. "I don't want no trouble either. And I still don't know what you mean by strange sounds." He weren't about to give in.

His cousin Darryl would be proud of him for lying to the police.

"Howls," Sheriff Thompson finally said. "Beastly howls on the wind. Like something's wounded, in pain, dying but not yet dead." He seemed angry.

"Don't got nothing like that out at my place," Franklin told the sheriff.

"Then you won't mind me coming out and taking a look at the place," the sheriff said.

"I would mind, Sheriff," Franklin said, his back stiffening. "You want to come out and look at my place, you get yourself a search warrant."

The sheriff narrowed his eyes at Franklin. "You sure that's how you want this to be?"

Franklin sighed, exasperated. "Look, there's nothing out there for you to see. There's nothing *nobody* can see."

Sheriff Thompson stroked his mustache, considering, before he nodded. "Y'all is talking about those damned ghosts again, aren't you. What'd they do this time?"

"Sheriff, I don't know what you mean," Franklin said. "Now, I ain't admitting to talking to ghosts. But if I was, believe me, these wouldn't be no ordinary ghosts."

"The ones howling? Then what's going on?" the sheriff growled.

"Nothing," Franklin said adamantly. "Nothing's going on. No ghosts is out at my place howling and making noise." No regular ghosts, at any rate.

"Fine," the sheriff said. "But if I get any more complaints, I will be getting that search warrant."

"It'll just be a waste of your time," Franklin said. And it would be. The sheriff couldn't see ghosts. No one could but him. But despite what all had happened the year before, the sheriff still didn't believe in ghosts. Still figured he'd be able to do something with Franklin's visitors.

"I've got my eye on you," the sheriff said, then he turned and walked back to his Crown Vic.

Franklin couldn't help himself. "Y'all have a nice day!" he called out.

He couldn't hear the sheriff muttering to himself in response, but he did imagine the sheriff had a few choice words for him in reply.

After Sheriff Thompson had driven off, Franklin slumped against a wall of the stand.

What was he going to do? How was he going to hush those howling ghosts?

FRANKLIN LEANED into the next kiss, his arms wrapped tightly around Julie. He wanted her in a way that he'd never wanted a woman before. She smelled wonderful, like freshly mowed grass and the lavender in her shampoo and her own, warm, womanly scent. He just wanted to hold her close and breathe in her smell along her neck, have it set his world on fire.

They'd had a nice night. He'd grilled steaks out in the backyard, and even eaten the green lettuce salad with the raspberry dressing she'd made without too many complaints. The howling ghosts had been quiet all evening. He hoped they wouldn't start up again until much, much later, like after midnight.

Franklin sat with Julie on the couch in the living room, and he was getting really comfy. And really uncomfortable too, at the same time, in his jeans.

He was glad he'd put on fresh sheets that morning.

They'd sat watching TV for a while, holding hands, until Julie had sighed and just snuggled up against him. She wore a white T-shirt with pretty lace around the scoop neck, tight enough to show the sliders on her bra straps and all her curves. Instead of her usual jeans, she'd worn a pair of light blue pants that Franklin had teased her about, reminding him of the scrubs she wore for work. Her soft brown hair had felt softer than ever in his hands, and her big hazel eyes sparkled in the dimly lit living room.

Franklin had enfolded her in his arms, started kissing her, and she'd started kissing back.

There weren't nothing better than this. Well, maybe a couple things.

Still, Franklin was in heaven, with Julie in his arms, fresh kisses between them, and the promise of a warm night ahead.

Franklin didn't notice anything was wrong until Julie pulled away. She shivered in his arms.

When Franklin tried to pull her closer again, Julie put a hand up in the center of his chest.

That made Franklin pay attention.

Damn it.

The ghosts had started howling again.

"What's that?" Julie asked, looking around the room.

"What's what?" Franklin asked. He leaned forward and snuck a kiss on Julie's neck, taking a quick breath of her scent and holding it.

"That. That sound," Julie said, shivering again.

Franklin sighed and sat back, giving up. For the moment. "I've got some strange ghosts visiting," he admitted.

"What do you mean?" Julie asked. She looked scared. "Has that creature from last year come back?"

"No, no, nothing like that thing." Franklin took hold of both of Julie's hands and brought them to his mouth, to kiss the back of each. He sighed.

"Out with it," Julie told him. "I had the feeling that something was wrong."

Franklin nodded. He hadn't wanted to burden Julie with his troubles.

"Two, three days before, I helped a man pass. He walked away from the backyard, out into the cornfield. I *know* he passed on. To whatever is next." Franklin paused. "Then he came back."

"How is that possible?" Julie asked.

The howling increased. The second ghost had joined in.

25

Franklin pulled Julie to his chest, settling her in there, his arms wrapped tightly around her. But he didn't try to kiss her again.

"I don't know," he said. "I'm not sure what's going on."

"That's why you was yawning all through dinner, isn't it?" Julie asked. "'Cause even you're having troubles sleeping through this racket."

Franklin nodded. "Yeah."

"So if they just came back, what will make them move on again?" Julie asked.

"I wish I knew," Franklin said. "A second one showed up this morning."

Julie nodded, her soft hair sliding across his chest. She shivered again as the ghosts howled louder. "You can tell me these sorts of things, you know," she said softly.

Franklin kissed her temple. "I know. It's just hard. I'm not used to telling anyone about the ghosts." Except Mama, but she didn't really count.

"I get it," Julie said. She pushed herself up, off Franklin's chest, then up off the couch, standing. She held her hand out to Franklin, helping him stand as well.

He knew better than to hope that she was gonna be leading him to the bedroom. Still his heart beat harder when she took his hand.

But she led him through the dining room, back out to the kitchen.

"I'd love to stay, but I just can't. Not with that kind of noise," Julie told him. She wrapped her arms around him, then stood on her tippy toes to kiss him lightly. "I'm sorry."

"I understand," Franklin said. They couldn't go to her place for the night—she had roommates. And he weren't about to suggest something as sordid as a hotel room. His mama raised him better than that.

Franklin walked Julie out to her car—a beat-up old Ford Focus with a specially tuned engine that could outrun most of the other cars on the highway.

He kissed her again, then opened the car door for her get in. The ghosts was out back, but he didn't want them getting any ideas or following her.

Julie started the engine then rolled down the window. "I know you said that using that knife from Eddie was cheatin'. But maybe you should think about it again."

Then she peeled up out of his driveway, spinning gravel before she hit the lane, driving away fast, as always.

Franklin thought for a moment. He'd forgotten about Eddie's blade. He'd given it to his cousin Darryl, for holding.

The blade was triangular, with three raised sides, made from a cold metal. Franklin wasn't sure what it was about that knife, but it weren't good.

Franklin wasn't quite sure what exactly that knife could do. He figured that it was a way to send a ghost to the beyond.

Mama had called it cheating. Instead of doing his duty and helping the ghost, it would have forced them away.

Would it kill a ghost? Or just…disperse it?

Franklin didn't want to have to use it on the ghosts who'd come back to haunt him.

They might not leave him a choice.

FRANKLIN GROGGILY SLAPPED at his alarm the next morning. The ghosts had kept him up most of the night.

When he checked outside, he swore.

Not only had they made so much racket they'd driven Julie away, they'd also started tearing up his corn. They hadn't destroyed the entire field, just flattened half a dozen stalks on the end.

How long before they destroyed everything growing in his yard?

Franklin shook his head. Damn it. Those ghosts weren't leaving him much choice.

He was going to have to go get that blade from his cousin Darryl.

Then maybe use it on his unwelcome guests.

CHAPTER 3

FRANKLIN DRAGGED his ass to the fruit and vegetable stand Saturday morning, dreading the day ahead. He was so tired he could barely see straight. The ghosts had really set up a racket all night right outside his bedroom window after Julie had left.

He was kind of glad she'd gone and hadn't had to listen to it.

Karl took one look at Franklin and gave a low whistle. "I don't want to hear about the good time you had with your girl last night. But man, you look like you was rode hard and put away wet."

Franklin nodded sheepishly. At least Karl had just given him a good excuse for being tired that day.

Not that he'd ever tell Karl the truth about the strange ghosts. It all felt like too much of a failure, somehow. He'd done his duty. What more was he supposed to do?

"You stay in the back of the stand as much as you can today," Karl instructed. "Just restock. Don't be trying to count change. Okay?"

"Thanks," Franklin said.

"And here," Karl added, thrusting a bottle of soda at Franklin.

Franklin grimaced at the taste. Too sweet, with a chemical burn in the aftertaste. But he'd forgotten to bring any of his own sweet tea.

And he did need the pick-me-up.

The teenage girls helping at the stand that day—Laticia and

Samantha—didn't make any smart remarks. But he caught them looking his way and giggling a couple of times.

Franklin was too tired to decide if it was better to be laughed at or called weird.

At the end of the day, Karl told him to skedaddle early. Franklin pedaled his bike into town instead of going straight home.

He was tempted to go to his old grocery store, but the store manager, Charlene, had never forgiven him, either for getting in trouble with the law or for Julie. So Franklin went to the fancy new pharmacy store up the hill from Main Street,.

He was going to sleep that night, ghosts be damned.

The store was only a couple months old. It had those annoying fluorescent lights that Franklin hated. The floor was wide open, just a big boxy space with row after row of low shelves.

At least the air conditioning was nice. For a while. Franklin suspected he'd freeze if he had to stay here for any length of time.

Franklin went straight to the section marked, "Sleep Aids." He found himself some orange, squishy earplugs, like the kind that Darryl had made him wear the one time they'd gone to the gun range. And he found three different types of sleep medicine. He was too tired to figure out which would work best for him, so he just bought all of them.

One of them was bound to do the job.

He paid cash for his goods, helping the girl behind the stand count out his change when the register didn't show it right.

It weren't that Franklin thought that the sheriff might be tracking him. But Franklin had seen too many TV shows where paying for something on credit was what brought the police to the criminal.

Though he wasn't a criminal. And it weren't really his fault. He'd done his duty, though part of him was starting to feel like he'd failed. Was there something more he was supposed to do?

Stupid ghosts.

Franklin tiredly pedaled back home. He merely glanced at his field, doing a quick count. After the first dozen stalks or so, the ghosts had stopped ravaging his field.

He hoped they wouldn't pick up where they'd left off. He still really wanted that blue ribbon prize for the best popping corn awarded by the Kentucky State Fair every year.

But he couldn't fight the ghosts. Not tonight.

Instead, Franklin picked at a bit of leftovers from the night before, even eating a bit more of the green lettuce salad that Julie had left for him.

As the sun went down and the ghosts picked up their howling, he found that the earplugs didn't really work. The sound pierced through them, straight to his soul, raising goose bumps all along his arms and across his back.

If he couldn't get them to shut up, at some point, he might have to try a pair of those fancy noise cancellation headphones that he'd seen on the TV.

Though that was just more money flying out the door.

Franklin tried to read the ingredients on the sleeping medicine, finally picking the one that was just pills, not the liquid that smelled too much like cough medicine.

Franklin didn't like how woozy the medicine made him feel. The room was spinning, like when he'd gone into shock after the creature had attacked him.

He weren't sure that taking the medicine were any better than listening to the ghosts howl.

In the morning, he didn't feel a whole lot better. Sure, he'd slept some. But it were, to use the phrase, the sleep of the dead, and he didn't feel rested.

More stalks of his corn had been trampled that night. What, had the ghosts been having a dance? They lay swirled on the ground.

Franklin shivered. The creature who'd attacked him the year before had looked like a whirlwind, with black whip-like arms made of thorns.

The creature hadn't come back. But there had been a wind out there, blowing last night, that Franklin had slept through.

Not tonight, though. Tonight, Franklin was gonna fetch that knife from Darryl. Just the prospect exhausted him. But he had to do something.

He weren't about to go a second year not competing with Karl for who grew the best popping corn. That just weren't right.

~

WHILE FRANKLIN WAS DRESSING for church that morning, putting on his good gray Sunday suit with the green shirt that both Julie and his cousin May liked, he thought seriously about calling May and asking for a ride.

Though she'd be happy to come and pick him up, or send her husband Henry after him if she was too tied up with the kids, she'd also insist on knowing all the particulars of why he wasn't feeling up to riding on his bicycle. It weren't too hot a day, and it weren't raining, either.

Franklin couldn't lie to May any more than he'd been able to lie to Mama. Maybe it was a woman thing. But he couldn't just tell her it was cause he felt like a ride that day.

Besides, he had to go talk with Darryl after church, and probably follow him home after dinner at Aunt Jasmine's. Best he have his own transportation and not be relying on others.

Franklin took his time pedaling to church. He always liked Sundays, riding along the quiet streets of Katherinesville, waving at folks just getting up themselves, at the kids playing in their yards. He took the pretty route, along the streets with the old oak trees growing and the colonial houses, made out of brick and solid.

If he'd had time, he might have driven by the Sorrel's place. But Franklin didn't like going by there as often anymore. After Adrianna died—killed by the creature—her husband Ray had seemed to have the wind knocked out of him. He'd always had white hair, but he'd been a hearty soul. Now, he seemed old.

Franklin still made a point of inviting Ray to dinner at least once a month. He was going to have to do that again in the next week or so.

That was, if he could quiet the ghosts at his place. Adrianna had been special, able to see lines of power in the very earth itself. Ray didn't need any reminders of that, of ghosts or special abilities.

The church itself was at the edge of town. It was a modern building. White stone went up to a tall arched roof, with plain glass in most of the windows, the fundraiser to replace them with stained glass ongoing. On the side were the classrooms, and back behind was the communal hall, where the youth ministry was serving donuts, cookies, homemade coffee cake, coffee, and sweet tea.

Franklin locked his bike to a bike stand on the side of the building, then decided to just go in the front. Miss Karen and Miss Kay stood outside, greeting everyone, a pair of spinster aunts who Franklin had thought were ancient when he'd been a boy.

They hadn't gotten any younger, but they hadn't gotten much older either. They'd both reached that ageless time, when they could be sixty or eighty, with as many smile-wrinkles as age-wrinkles around their eyes, their dark skin not showing any age spots.

They both had white hair, neatly trimmed, that had been allowed to kink naturally. Miss Karen had a small pink hat pinned carefully to her hair, while Miss Kay wore a bright yellow sun hat. They were smartly dressed in their Sunday best with matching gloves, of course.

"Good morning, Franklin," said Miss Karen.

"Nice to see you, young man," said Miss Kay, not to be outdone.

"Morning, ladies," Franklin said, nodding to them. He didn't usually wear a hat, but he'd been thinking that maybe he needed a church-going hat. Not his Stetson, but something similar.

"It's gonna be a hot one, today," Miss Karen told him.

"Though it's supposed to rain tomorrow," Miss Kay added.

"Thank you," Franklin said gravely. "I'll keep that in mind."

He stepped into the cool nave. Red tile made up the floor. The door to the sanctuary arched up, made from a pale wood. The greeters—Mr. and Mrs. Smith, a younger couple, just recently joined the church—handed him a program.

Quiet organ music filled the sanctuary, something soothing. Light-colored wooden beams lifted the peaked roof, as if raising it closer to God. Franklin had always liked the openness of the sanctuary, how the aisle running down the center was wide enough for three lines of folks. The cross at the front was carved out of dark wood, and the same dark wood made up the pulpit.

Franklin spotted his cousin Jason sitting toward the back, where he generally sat, with his two girls, Lisa and Karen.

Jason's wife Elise wasn't there again.

The girls' dresses were clean and pressed, but it looked as though Lisa, the youngest, had done her own hair, the ends all pulled up into an uneven ponytail, though someone had tried to pretty it up with a bright red bow.

He couldn't imagine Elise letting the girls go to church like that. What was going on with her?

But Jason wouldn't say, had even gotten huffy and left the one time Darryl had asked outright.

No one in the family could help Jason until he asked for help. They'd all offered, only to be told there weren't no problem, and to leave him alone. He'd even threatened to stop coming to Sunday dinners.

Then again, Franklin understood where Jason was coming from. He hated asking for help from anyone as well.

Particularly with ghosts and things that no one in his family really understood.

"Howdy," Franklin said, coming up and sitting behind his cousin. Jason wore a good Sunday suit as well, light brown with a white shirt.

"Morning, Cuz," Jason said, turning around in his seat and shaking Franklin's hand. He held on for a moment, really looking at Franklin. "You okay?" he asked quietly.

"Just tired," Franklin assured him. And really. There weren't anything Jason could do. Franklin was just going to have to talk with Darryl.

"You seen Darryl?" Franklin asked as he got settled in.

"They won't be here this morning," Lisa said breathlessly. "They had to go to the hospital!"

"What happened?" Franklin asked, frowning.

Jason chuckled. "Fool went out hot rodding on his new bike, showing it off for the kids."

"Who, Tommy?" Darryl's eldest had recently turned twelve and felt as though he no longer had to listen to any of the adults.

"Nope. Darryl," Jason said, still chuckling. "Broke his arm."

Franklin gave his own chuckle. "Really?" he asked. Seemed like something his cousin would do, though. He was the oldest of them, six years older than Franklin, who was the youngest.

"Yeah. We'll be going over there for Sunday dinner," Jason said. "Didn't May call you?"

Franklin sheepishly shrugged. "Didn't check my phone for messages," he admitted. Had he been so tired that he hadn't heard it? What if Julie had left him a message? When he pulled it out of his pocket and flipped it open, he saw he had both a voicemail as well as a text message.

"Why you got such an old phone, Uncle Franklin?" Lisa asked.

"'Cause I don't barely use it," Franklin said. He didn't need something fancy that could take pictures and play music and connect to the internet. He could send text messages on his little phone, but it was hard, having to press through all the keys to get to the right letter.

The text message from May was typically brief: *Sunday dinner at Darryls.* He assumed the voicemail would say the same, though maybe offering him a ride, too.

He'd have to remember to send a note to Julie, later.

"There you are," May said from behind Franklin.

She twhapped him on the shoulder.

"Ow," Franklin said, turning to see her.

She looked good, though that yellow dress she was wearing was too tight, and the length was barely appropriate for church. She wore her hair short on the sides and tall on top. Franklin recognized the style as something Mama would do for short women like May.

May got her three kids settled, Franklin shaking hands with Henry, her husband, just as the prelude music came to an end. As Franklin was about to stand up with the congregation and sing the first hymn, May gripped his shoulder hard.

"We gotta talk," she whispered urgently into his ear.

Franklin cast a worried look over his shoulder. Was there something going on with his cousin? She looked fine, though, her broad eyes clear, her brown skin healthy. She was the only one of them to have his mama's nose, flat and wide, with an equally wide mouth.

May, however, just made a shooing motion with her hand, getting him to turn back around and face the front.

What did she want? There weren't ghosts haunting her too, were there?

Franklin would just have to wait until the end of the service to find out.

～

FRANKLIN SPENT most of the sermon disagreeing in his head with Preacher Sinclair. It weren't that the preacher were a bad man. He'd even tried to help the one time Franklin and Darryl had gone out after the creature the year before.

But the preacher didn't always see things like Franklin did, and not just ghosts. Where he'd come up with the notion that folks was frail, Franklin didn't know. Even the most timid of folks would turn and stand up and fight if they was pushed too far.

The preacher had his own demons, his own depression to battle. Maybe that was why he felt that only God could help him.

While Franklin believed in the power of prayer, and knew that God worked miracles, folks also needed to help themselves.

The phrase that caught Franklin this time was "how death comes for us all."

But what if it don't? Or what if death weren't the final end? What if there was more?

Franklin just didn't know, and it hurt his head going round and round about such things.

At the end of the sermon, though, Franklin still shook the preacher's hand and told him it was good.

It had made Franklin think, and he figured that was the point, even if he weren't thinking along the same lines that the preacher wanted him to.

Jason offered to put Franklin's bike in the back of his Suburban and to give Franklin a ride to Darryl's. Aunt Jasmine was already there, helping Georgia, Darryl's wife, with the boys.

Franklin accepted, particularly when he saw May making a beeline toward him.

It weren't that he was avoiding his cousin. He knew that was impossible. He still wanted to put off the inevitable.

Franklin played "I spy" with the girls on the drive out to Darryl's. They both knew their letters real good, but Franklin was better at "spying" things.

Darryl's brand new black pickup sat in the driveway, Aunt Jasmine's old green Ford beside it. Franklin knew that when Lexine had died, she'd left a will, and Aunt Jasmine had inherited a bunch of money. He'd thought she'd be the one buying a new car.

Jason pulled up behind the truck, then waited while Franklin pulled his bike out of the back.

"I'd be happy to give you a ride home," Jason told Franklin quietly as he walked his bike up the driveway.

"Naw, I'm probably going to hang out for a while tonight," Franklin said.

Jason nodded. "You and Darryl aren't getting into trouble again, are you? Like last year?"

Franklin opened his mouth, then closed it again. "I sure hope not," he said fervently.

"You ever need anything, you let me know," Jason told Franklin. "I mean it."

Franklin turned to face Jason. "I could say the same thing to you, Jason," he said quietly. "If you need help with the girls…"

Jason sighed. "Maybe…Maybe next week. You should come by. With that girlfriend of yours," he added with a sly grin.

"I'll find out what her work schedule will be next week and give you a call," Franklin promised.

And he would.

It was nice to know that his family was worried about him, and would support him as well, even if they didn't quite know what it was that he did with the ghosts.

It was also nice to be able to support them in return.

~

MAY DIDN'T corner Franklin until after supper, when he was fetching Darryl another sweet tea from the kitchen.

"Okay," May said, stepping into the doorway leading to the living room. "Spill."

"What do you mean?" Franklin asked, taking a step back.

He'd taken off his suit jacket, but he was still in his good green shirt and dress slacks. May had changed completely, wearing a black-and-white striped top that would have looked better on a teenager, as well as tight jeans that looked sprayed on.

"You look as pale as those ghosts you see," May told him. "Now, don't try to lie to me. I know you better. I seen you last year, when you been injured. And I know you ain't sick. You ain't never been sick a day in your life. So what gives?"

Franklin took a step back at her onslaught, but smiled. May was pure fierceness, as much a force of nature as Mama had been.

"It's nothing," Franklin said with a casual shrug.

"You don't have girl troubles or something, do you?" May asked. "You and Julie still doing all right?"

"We're fine," Franklin assured her, though they wouldn't be if he didn't take care of this ghost problem.

"You sure?" May asked, peering closely. "'Cause something's going on with you. Oh lord. You haven't made her pregnant, have you?"

"No, ma'am," Franklin said, horrified. He wouldn't just get Julie pregnant, then leave her. She'd assured him that she was on birth control and they didn't have anything to worry about.

"Kids ain't the end of the world, you know," May said, her tone softening. "Your whole life changes, but that's just part of the fun." She looked Franklin up and down critically. "You ever gonna have any kids of your own?"

Franklin shrugged. He'd been thinking more about that since he got himself a serious girlfriend. But it was too soon for that kind of thing.

"All right. I know something's up. And you're as stubborn as a pregnant ass when it comes to talking about these things. Worse than Jason. I swear. Men."

May turned to go, then turned back. "But honey, if you need anything, or you need to talk with someone, you know your family's here, right?"

"I do," Franklin said fervently. "And thank you."

May gave him a soft smile before she marched back out to the living room to make sure that her own three hellions continued to play nice.

Franklin wondered how he'd got so lucky to have such a good family. That was something that he was thankful for, and he didn't need no preacher to tell him that.

AFTER JASON and May had left with their respective broods in tow, Franklin asked Darryl, "Can I talk with you for a minute?"

Darryl nodded warily. His arm was in a white cast, held in place by a black sling across his chest. The kids had all signed it. Little Shanna had even put a pink sparkly-heart sticker on it. "Let's go out to the garage," he suggested.

He stood up slowly from the couch, obviously in pain. He'd dislocated his shoulder and fractured his forearm, putting his hand out to stop himself from falling at high speed. He'd joked weakly about the other guy, but Franklin could tell his heart wasn't in it.

The garage was cool, filled with the chill of the night. It smelled like fresh car oil and shaved metal. Darryl flipped a light on over his workbench. He had more tools than Franklin could name, all neatly arranged, hanging on the wall. Beside the workbench stood a metal blue-and-gray toolbox that was almost as big as Franklin's dresser.

Darryl walked directly to the small refrigerator under the bench, pulling out a beer, then offering one to Franklin.

"Ain't you supposed to only be drinking tea while you're on the pain meds?" Franklin asked, shaking his head.

Darryl grinned at him. "Little beer ain't gonna hurt. So what's up? You been sitting there long-faced all night. Got girl trouble?"

"No, I ain't got girl trouble. Why does everyone assume that's what's wrong?" Franklin asked, exasperated.

"'Cause it's fun to get you riled up," Darryl said. He leaned his butt against the workbench. "So what's up?"

Franklin took a deep breath. "You remember that knife I asked you to hold for me?"

Darryl straightened up. "Yes, I do."

What had Darryl all serious all of a sudden?

"I need it back," Franklin said plainly.

Darryl shook his head. "No, you don't. Not until you explain why." He took a long drink from his beer, looking away into the shadows. "It ain't a good thing. That blade's haunted or something. I ain't saying it's evil, but it ain't good."

"I know," Franklin said. "And I wouldn't ask you for it if I didn't think I really needed it."

"Needed it?" Darryl turned back to stare hard at Franklin. "Need it for what?"

"Ghosts been coming back. After they've passed," Franklin finally admitted.

"So?" Darryl asked. "Help them pass again."

"They're not…they're not like regular ghosts."

"They tearing things up?" Darryl asked.

Franklin wondered what Darryl thought he could do about it. It weren't like the ghosts were hiding somewhere and needed to be hunted down.

"A little," Franklin said. "Mostly, they's howling. Making an awful racket. Can't sleep."

"That's why you're so tired looking," Darryl said, nodding. "I kept telling 'em that you'd been having too much fun with your girl."

"Thanks," Franklin said, though he weren't sure being thought of as a hound dog was much better.

Darryl just grinned at Franklin, but didn't say anything more.

"These ghosts—they can't tell me their *intent*. They're lost here. I don't know how to help them pass. And I got to get some sleep," Franklin said. "The neighbors are starting to complain. Plus, they scared Julie away the other night."

"I see how it is," Darryl said with a leer.

"Oh please," Franklin said, rolling his eyes.

Darryl grew serious again. "I understand you need something. But ain't there something else? You don't know how that knife will twist your soul."

"Did you use it?" Franklin asked, curious. Because Darryl hadn't seemed like he'd changed at all.

"Nope. Not once," Darryl said. "I did take it out with me, hunting, one time," he said. "Now, you might accuse me of making stuff up. And hell, maybe it was all in my imagination. But that blade wanted blood. And pain. It ain't good."

"I know," Franklin said. He still had to try it. He had to do *something*. "But I got to help these ghosts pass. It's my duty. Even if they don't know how to leave this world. I got to help them."

"And you think the knife will do that? Force the ghosts into Heaven?" Darryl asked.

"Or something," Franklin said, nodding.

Darryl sighed, took a long swig from his beer. "I don't like this," he said.

"I don't like it either," Franklin told him. But he was desperate tired. It was the only thing his poor brain could think of.

Darryl nodded. "Okay then. Let's go get the knife. But you don't have to keep it, if you don't want to. Don't have to use it."

"Where is it?" Franklin asked. He'd assumed that Darryl would have kept it in the gun safe, locked away. "You didn't give it to someone else to keep, did you?"

"Hell no," Darryl said. He walked over to the side of the garage and tried to get down a shovel hanging there.

Franklin hurried over to help, taking the shovel in both hands.

"And can you grab those as well?" Darryl said, pointing at a set of long-handled clippers.

"Where the hell is the knife?" Franklin asked, perplexed.

"I couldn't keep it out here. It…it…I could hear it, okay? And I was afraid of how it might influence the kids," Darryl said, angry.

"You should have given it back to me then," Franklin told him quietly. "I would have held it."

Though Franklin had also found the knife disquieting. He'd thought Darryl, though, would have been immune to it.

Darryl shook his head. "You asked me to hold onto it for you. I figured it was louder for you. So I buried it. In the backyard."

Franklin looked down at his good dress pants. Damn it. He wasn't prepared to do some kind of yard work.

Darryl mutely pointed to a pair of overalls.

Franklin pulled them down, grumbling. He had a feeling that he wasn't going to like this.

Not one bit.

CHAPTER 4

"WHAT ARE you two fools doing out there?" Georgia, Darryl's wife, called from the back door.

"Franklin here's gonna take care of that nasty thorn bush," Darryl assured her.

"In the middle of the night?" she asked.

"No time like the present, ma'am," Franklin replied respectfully.

"I don't know what you two are up to. Just don't hurt yourself," she said, slamming the door shut.

Franklin looked dourly at the massive thorn bush. While he thought Georgia's sentiment was good advice, he weren't sure he could follow it.

The overgrown thorn bush lurked in the far corner of Darryl's backyard. In the dim light, it reminded Franklin of the creature he'd fought the year before, massive and deadly, with nasty thorns hungry for his flesh.

"Why'd you bury the knife under this thing?" Franklin asked. The long-handled clippers would help, but he needed gloves lined with steel to protect his hands from those thorns.

"Didn't," Darryl said. "Bush grew up over the knife. Practically overnight. Never seen something grow so fast before. Not even your special popping corn."

"Well, hell," Franklin said.

"Trimmed it back regularly," Darryl added. "Didn't slow it down one bit. Even tried burning it, once. Damned branches are too green. Hot enough fire to take it out would also take out the fence."

Franklin nodded. He'd bet that Darryl had wanted to try it anyway, and Georgia had told him just what kind of fool she thought he was.

"You try sprinkling some holy water or something on it?" Franklin asked. The plant wasn't necessarily evil. But it had an awareness that he didn't like.

"No," Darryl said slowly. "Do you think I should?"

Franklin shrugged, knowing the motion would be lost in the darkness. "Maybe after we pull it up."

"You sure you want to dig up that blade?" Darryl asked.

Franklin sighed. He needed to do something about the ghosts haunting him. Plus, now he felt bad for asking Darryl to hold it for him.

"I'll deal with it," Franklin promised. He wasn't sure if he wanted to try to give it back to Eddie after he finished using it. Or where he'd put it after he was done with it.

He sure didn't want nasty vines like this taking over his fields.

But that was a problem for another day. Right now, he had enough of a fight ahead of him with the damned thorn bush.

When Darryl made to reach for the clippers, Franklin held them out of reach. "What the hell do you think you're doing?"

"I was aiming to help," Darryl said patiently, as though he was trying to explain something to May's youngest.

"You're already injured," Franklin told him. "And while I wouldn't care too much if you decided to be an idiot and hurt yourself again, I don't need first Georgia, then May, tearing strips from *my* hide over it."

They stood glaring at each other for a moment, before Darryl shrugged and said, "Have it your way, then."

"Good," Franklin said. "Now the way you can help is to shine that big ol' flashlight of yours on the bush so I can see what I'm doing."

"Sure thing, boss," Darryl said.

Franklin ignored the insult. It was just Darryl being Darryl, calling him by a white man's term.

Darryl's light set the thorn bush into stark contrast. The branches stretched out on either side from the corner, like it was preparing for a deadly embrace. It looked frozen in time and space, like a criminal that had just been caught by a prison spotlight. It had an air to it, though, like it was just waiting for some fool to come along and challenge it.

Franklin gave a low whistle. The thorns was three inches long, with hundreds of shorter thorns circling each limb.

It didn't shrink back as Franklin approached with the clippers. That was just his imagination.

Franklin took another step forward, reaching for one of the near branches.

"Watch it," Darryl warned suddenly.

Franklin stepped back, out of reach as one of the branches suddenly whipped around, aiming for him.

"Did you see that?" Franklin asked, turning toward Darryl.

"It must have been the wind. Or something," Darryl said, looking uncomfortable.

Franklin snorted. "Yeah. The wind." The evening was completely still, without even the promise of a breeze to come.

Franklin hoisted his clippers in front of him, like a knight with a shield. Then he darted forward, clipping one branch and jumping back. Then the next. He danced away before he tried for a third, Darryl warning him again.

Slowly, Franklin sheared the bush of its deadly limbs, only getting caught once on the arm and once on the side. He knew both points were infected, and he'd need some kind of antibiotic gel on them before he went to bed.

Franklin realized, too late, that the limbs he'd trimmed from the bush now lay like their own barrier, a massive wall of thorny branches. Any time Franklin tried to pick one up, even with the leather gloves, the thorns reached through and pricked his hands.

He let Darryl help a little then, kicking the branches away enough until Franklin could finally get at the trunk of the bush.

The clippers Franklin was using weren't wide enough—or sharp enough—to give him enough leverage to hack all the way through the trunk.

"Leave it," Darryl said.

"You think it'll just let me dig up its roots without falling over or trying to impale me?" Franklin asked, exasperated.

Then he stopped and looked at Darryl. Even in the dim light, and with Darryl's dark skin, Franklin could still see how ragged he looked, his skin taking on a coating of ash.

"Dude. Go to bed. I got this," Franklin assured his cousin, walking over to him and taking the flashlight from his hands.

Darryl shook his head. "No, no. I can do this."

"You got a broken arm. We're through the worst of it. All I got to do now is dig," Franklin pointed out. "You don't need to stay here. You can go to bed. Get some rest. Get yourself out of pain. Before Georgia, and then May, come and yell at me."

Darryl gave Franklin a weak grin. "They would yell at you too, wouldn't they?"

"That they would, Cuz," Franklin said solemnly.

"It don't feel right, leaving you to fight this thing on your own," Darryl said.

"It ain't got much fight left in it," Franklin assured him, though he was afraid the bush was playing possum again.

"You sure?" Darryl asked, swaying as he stood.

"I'm sure," Franklin said firmly. "Go to bed."

"You just holler, you need anything," Darryl said, turning and yawning hugely.

Franklin nodded, though he was determined not to ask for more help.

He could fight this damned thorn bush on his own.

How bad could it be?

～

FRANKLIN HAD BEEN RIGHT. The bush *had* been playing possum. As soon as he shone the light on it, he realized there were more branches, hidden in the back.

He was exposing himself by getting close enough to trim them. They'd whip around for certain, lash his back, maybe his face.

Instead of continuing with his front attack, Franklin cleared out one of the sides and started attacking from there. Though the branches tried to slide out of the way, he kept attacking the main stalk, until it was bare.

But not defenseless.

Franklin took the shovel next. He stood still for a moment, feeling the full night wrapping around him. It wasn't as peaceful here. Neighbors sat on the other side of the fence. But Georgia wouldn't let Darryl move them all the way out of town—she wanted a safer place for the kids to play, and not as long of a trek to their schools.

It wasn't that the neighbors were making noise. But Franklin still knew they were there. He shook his head. They weren't taking his air. It just kind of felt like that sometimes, in closed-in spaces. But his frustration was building, tearing apart the peace that normally filled Franklin.

Damn it. He needed that knife. And then he needed to sleep for a month.

With a silent scream, Franklin hefted the shovel and brought it down, bashing the side of the thorn bush.

He could almost *feel* the bush's surprise. It hadn't been expecting that at all.

Franklin went to the other side and bashed it as well, breaking off the thorns still bristling from the trunk.

It weren't enough to merely bend them down. The bush was wily. It could make those thorns spring up again.

But Franklin breaking them fully off—well, it would take some time for the bush to recover from that.

Time Franklin didn't intend to give it.

Finally, Franklin had pushed enough of the vines out of the way, bashed off enough of the thorns, that he felt like he could start digging.

Of course, the roots of the thorn bush were prickled with thorns as well. Not as sharp as the ones above ground. But the roots wove together in a hard thorny ball, making it difficult for Franklin to break the ground and really dig in.

He wouldn't be denied, though. He wished he had his digging pole. He should have asked Darryl for one.

But wishes weren't fishes...something Mama used to say.

Franklin kept digging, jumping out of the way when the branches above him creaked.

Damned bush was trying to make another attack. Franklin bashed it with his shovel, panting and sweating hard in the cool evening.

He might have to call Karl and take Monday off, at this rate.

Finally, Franklin dug down deep enough to see the blade, glittering darkly at the heart of the root ball.

Franklin reached out with his hands, then hesitated.

Too many thorns.

But he couldn't break the root ball apart with his shovel. It was too springy. The blade of the shovel just bounced off

Franklin stepped back, considering. Maybe he could clip at the roots with the clipper, but that would take forever. And the root mass was more likely to grow back together, and the bush itself was poised for another attack.

What could he use instead?

Franklin raised the flashlight, turning and looking through the yard. What else was there? What could he use?

On the far side of the yard, on its back with the wheels up in the air, was the culprit of Darryl's injury, the new mountain bike.

Sorry, Darryl, Franklin whispered as he stalked across the yard.

The bike chain came off easily enough, particularly when Franklin popped one of the link pins. The front tire came off as well, merely clipped on, a modern design that Franklin didn't approve of.

He'd have to talk to Darryl about his choice of bicycle later.

Armed with familiar parts, Franklin swaggered back across the yard. "So you think you're bad?" he sneered.

He realized if any of the neighbors looked outside at this point, they'd think he was crazy.

Then again, most of the people in Katherinesville who were merely acquainted with him and his talking to ghosts already thought he was crazy.

"You're nothing," Franklin sneered. "You can't reach me and you can't hurt me. And I'm well on my way to *annihilating* you."

The remains of the thorn bush trembled, but not in fear.

A dare.

Do your worst.

Franklin lashed out with the bicycle chain. It whipped around the top of the bush, then he yanked it away, shredding vegetation as he untangled it.

Then he had to duck. Thorns loosed by the chain flew toward him. One caught him in the shoulder.

"That's it," Franklin said. He looped the bicycle chain through the wheel, then whirled it over his head, like some kind of ancient discus. He bashed into the bush again and again, knocking it to one side, then the other. He pushed the bush further back, making it tilt.

As it pulled back, the root ball holding the knife came closer and closer to the surface.

Finally, when the handle of the blade had cleared the hole, Franklin whirled the tire one last time, letting go of one end of the chain at the same time.

The wheel spun as it flew through the air, the tire already badly punctured and the spokes bent. It bashed straight into the bush, making it shiver. Then it hung there, like some kind of modern art, a tire sacrificed for y'all's sins.

With the bush distracted by the tire, Franklin used the chain to whip the ball root holding the knife, tearing it away from the main roots.

With a daring leap, Franklin snatched the blade from the ball root, then hurriedly leaped out of the way again, before the thorn bush could make another grab for him.

Franklin stood panting in the center of the yard. He bled from half a dozen scratches, his shoulder ached from where the one thorn had imbedded itself, and it felt to him as though the knife still pulsed, evilly, in his hand.

The thorn bush slumped over, defeated. Its branches lay abandoned on the ground, no longer a deadly barrier.

Franklin still didn't trust it. He left the wheel there, where it was, hanging from the single trunk. It wouldn't surprise him if the bush grew more branches overnight, just so it could tear the wheel apart.

Somehow, Franklin didn't think Darryl would be riding his bike again anytime soon.

After collecting up the other tools and putting them on the steps next to the back door, Franklin let himself out the side gate.

He had a long bike ride home that he wasn't looking forward to. And his own ghosts to deal with once he got there.

He was definitely gonna take a day off next week.

Franklin put the blade in one of the leg pockets of his overalls, buttoning it carefully, making sure that it was secure. It wouldn't do now for him to just lose the thing.

Though the way the knife *pushed* at him, trying to make its intent clear, he weren't sure if that wasn't just the best thing for it. For it to be lost, buried, out of sight.

But he'd started down this path. And he didn't know of any other way to get rid of his unwelcome guests.

He just hoped Mama would forgive him for what he was about to do.

FRANKLIN PUSHED his bike into his shed, exhausted. It had seemed as though he'd felt every single bump in the road coming home. He'd known that the thorns on that damned bush had probably been tainted with something—he just hoped it weren't poisonous.

Sweet Bess glared at Franklin from the corner of the house, but he couldn't pay her no mind. He had to get inside. Get some rest.

He pulled out his phone and flipped it open. It was gonna take him forever to send Karl a text message, pressing each key carefully until it reached the right letter.

But he didn't see how he'd get himself up again in only four—no, three and a half hours, by now. Plus, though the ghosts were quieter, he could still hear 'em moaning something fierce out back.

Franklin slowly climbed the two steps up to the porch, still pressing buttons on his phone. "Dang it," he said when he realized he would have to redo the last word. It had all come out garbled.

He unlocked his door and stepped inside, still focused on his phone, grateful for the light.

Wait.

Light?

Franklin looked up.

Someone had dragged his kitchen table out from the corner where it usually sat and placed it in the center of the kitchen floor. An odd, yellowish glow came from the center of it, like a sickly mist.

A white man dressed in blue surgical scrubs stood behind the table. He wore a doctor's mask across his face, and a blue cap over his head. He waved his hands across the table, in and out of the yellow glow, as if he were one of those fancy orchestra conductors.

"What are you doing?" Franklin asked, confused. That weren't no ghost standing there, or some kind of creature from Franklin's exhausted imagination.

"Waiting for you, Franklin," the man said. His voice was smooth and educated. He took a loud breath. "Now, watch."

The man continued his conducting, moving his hands out toward the edges of the table then scooping them together, like he was raising armfuls of leaves. The glow spread out, growing long across the top of the table.

More mist rose up, darker mist. It started collecting itself into a shape.

A human shape.

"What are you doing?" Franklin asked, horrified. He tried moving forward to stop the man, but he found himself moving sluggishly slow, as if the mist had wrapped around his ankles and had tied him there.

Franklin reached down to see if he could free himself.

He still had his phone in his hand.

The mist was freezing his bones. It was hard to think, hard to move.

Franklin typed out "9-1-1" and hit send.

Would Karl get the text in time? Would he understand that Franklin needed help?

Franklin pulled himself back up straight slowly. At least the man behind the table hadn't seemed to notice Franklin's call. He was focused on the mist, pushing it together, making it more solid. Sweat dropped freely from his forehead.

Whatever the hell he was doing, it was taking an awful lot out of him.

Finally, he seemed satisfied with his work. He lifted his hands up above his head and called out in some foreign language.

It weren't a friendly language. The man gargled and hissed, the words wrapped around his tongue like thorns.

Franklin shivered. It was like the doctor was invoking an evil spirit to come down and witness his work.

Something unholy.

The form on the table solidified more, changing shape, growing breasts and hips and a recognizable face.

Mama.

Franklin had heard the phrase before about "a body at rest." And that's what Mama looked like—a body at complete rest. She was at peace.

Then her eyes opened.

Franklin had to smile when that familiar glare was immediately directed at him. Then it fixed on the stranger.

But then Mama's eyes started changing. Hollowing out. Growing dark and black and empty.

"Stop!" Franklin said.

The man was bringing back Mama's ghost, like he'd brought back the others. The ones who was still howling in Franklin's backyard.

But it wouldn't be Mama. Not really. It would look like her, but Franklin could already see the life being drained out of her.

Not that a ghost had that much life to start with. All her will was being taken away, just leaving her with the anger of being ripped out of Heaven.

"You don't want to see your mother?" the man asked, his voice dripping with false concern. "What kind of a son are you?"

"Don't you mess with my mama," Franklin warned. "You put her back." How dare he? It just weren't right, messing with the dead like he was doing.

It was why the ghosts who'd returned to haunt Franklin had seemed unnatural. The man had brought them back against their will, against nature.

The man seemed to consider for a moment before nodding and saying, "All right. I'll stop the process, scoot her back beyond. But I'm going to need something for my efforts."

That right there stopped Franklin cold. "What?" he asked, though he had an idea.

"That blade you carry so thoughtlessly in your pocket," the man said.

Greed filled the man's beady eyes.

Franklin did *not* want to give this man the knife. It was a dangerous thing. Not evil, but not good.

What would this man…this *magician*…do with such a powerful tool?

"Make up your mind," the man warned. "I can only hold her like this for so long. Then she slips into awareness, comes back to this plane."

Mama didn't have enough of herself to throw an effective glare at the man.

But Franklin didn't have to hear her actually howl to know what she would sound like, how awful it would be. It would tear him to pieces. While he might miss her something fierce, it wouldn't be the same.

Mama might not be happy with Franklin for handing over the blade to this man, but she'd *never* forgive him for allowing her to be brought back, her will not her own.

Franklin slowly unzipped the pocket on his thigh where the blade had been resting, heavy and cold. It didn't seem repelled by the man, though Franklin was equally sure the blade kinda liked where it was, being held by Franklin.

Could Franklin just throw it at the man? Would it cut him? Or would it just go gliding into his hand, as if it were made to be there?

What the hell was this blade? What kind of spirits made up its essence? Why was it giving Franklin all these thoughts and feelings?

The doctor seemed to know—he knew all kinds of things about the knife, Franklin would bet. Probably had been studying it for some time.

The man gestured for Franklin to come closer. Franklin didn't want to go. Damn it, he *hated* being bullied.

But Mama didn't have a lot of time, or she'd be *stuck* here, howling like the other spirits.

Franklin took two shuffling steps forward. Again, he hesitated. He couldn't run—the mists held him too tightly for him to do much than just shuffle along. Turning the blade on himself didn't make no sense either: he'd just end up dying and the doctor would take the knife anyway.

With a suffering sigh, Franklin raised his arm and reached over the table where Mama still lay, her glare losing more power as her will dribbled away, handing this dangerous, far too *aware* blade over to a madman.

"You did the right thing, son," the man said solemnly. "You'll see. Everyone in the whole world will see. You'll be sung of as a hero. Just as the knife will be praised for playing its part."

Was this guy drunk or something? What was he talking about?

"The world will be a much better place. You mark my words," the doctor said, running his fingers carefully along the blade of the knife, turning it to see all three prongs.

Mama started fading immediately, her eyes losing their haunted stare and going back to normal. She shook her head at Franklin, disapproving of what he'd just done.

Franklin hoped she'd understand some as well.

"Goodbye, Mama," Franklin said softly.

When Franklin looked back up, the man was already on his side of the table. He smelled of sour sweat and burnt sage, like what Lexine had used when calming her spirits.

"You've got your phone with you?" the man inquired.

Franklin told the man, "No," though he still had it in his other hand.

"I can see it right there," the man said. "Good."

He moved faster than Franklin had anticipated, as fast as the vines he'd fought earlier.

Just as suddenly, the knife was in Franklin's side. The blade seared cold into Franklin's body. He stumbled against the table, the pain in his side making the room waver.

"Why'd you do that for?" Franklin asked.

"Call 911," the man instructed. "They have a response time of nine-point-two minutes in this county."

Franklin reached for his phone but he couldn't get his fingers to work.

"It's okay if you do die," the man told him just before he walked out the door. "I'll just use your soul too."

Hell if Franklin was going to let that happen.

He kept trying to press buttons when suddenly the phone in his hand rang.

Did he do that?

He managed to press the "On" button.

"Hello?" he said. He was impressed by how normal his voice sounded.

"What the hell is going on out there?" Karl yelled.

"I been stabbed," Franklin said. He was losing his grip on the table.

That was okay. It was much better down on the ground.

Oh. Or even more better outside.

"Franklin—Franklin!"

Karl's voice sounded tinny and far away.

"I'm here. Going outside," Franklin added.

If he were gonna die, it was gonna be in his cornfields.

Hopefully they'd find his hat and bury him in that too. As well as his good Sunday suit. And maybe the green shirt that both Julie and his cousin May liked.

"You ain't dying. Not until I come and personally kick your ass," Karl said. "I've already called 911. They should be on their way."

"In nine-point-two minutes," Franklin said.

The door was already open. Franklin pulled himself outside.

He felt as if he could breathe, finally, though the pain in his side made it hard. He rolled over onto his back, his head on the edge of the porch, just so he could see the stars.

Franklin weren't afraid to die. He'd done his best. Even Mama would say that he deserved his peace.

Was that sirens in the distance? Or just the cycling of the cicadas?

Franklin took as deep a breath as he could and closed his eyes.

If only he could have seen Julie one more time.

CHAPTER 5

Franklin felt as though sand glued his eyes shut. He scrunched them tighter, before finally prying them open.

First thing he saw were the white walls of the hospital. A white curtain hung on his right, separating his bed from the next. He wiggled his toes under the white blanket.

Oh dear lord. *That* was a mistake. Just that little movement woke up the rest of his body. *Everything* hurt. From his fingernails up to the roots of his hair, down his shins. Even the soles of his feet.

He'd been stabbed, right? Franklin thought about it, trying to feel the wound.

It felt…different. Like there was still a part of the knife stuck inside him, a hard line of silver pain.

That damned idiot hadn't come back and stabbed him a second time, had he?

But Franklin couldn't find any other parts of his body that hurt like the knife wound.

He was reaching for the nurse's call button, to get someone to tell him what the hell had happened, when Julie came bursting in. She was in regular clothes, not her nurse scrubs, a snug-fitting purple T-shirt that would have made Mama frown and jeans. Her soft brown hair was mussed, like she'd been in a hurry that morning. She looked nice, her eyes more green than brown.

Franklin couldn't help the happiness bubbling up inside him at the sight of her. "Hey darling," he said, reaching out his hand for hers.

Julie took his hand, then leaned over and kissed his dry lips. She smelled wonderful and womanly.

Not that he was in any shape to do anything about it.

Huh. It might really be love if he felt like that about her even when the rest of him felt like he'd been dragged along three miles of gravel road.

When Julie straightened up, she fixed Franklin with a glare.

Where'd Julie learn to do that? To make him feel so guilty with just with a look? Or was it a woman thing? That now Mama, May, and Julie all knew?

"I don't *ever* want to find you here again. I mean it, Franklin Kanly," Julie said. She held onto his hand when he would have pulled it away. "You scared me silly when I got the call that you was here."

"Sorry," Franklin said. Though it wasn't really his fault. It weren't as though he stabbed himself.

"I got stabbed. By that blade. Eddie's knife," Franklin said. The line of hard metal pain in his side flared at the mention of it. "What the hell is that thing? What was it made for? Do y'all know the history of it?"

Julie shrugged. "I don't know. Eddie's always had it. Used it as a power focus for the group, when we were praying and chanting."

"We need to talk to Eddie," Franklin said.

"Okay," Julie said, nodding. Then she grinned. "Road trip."

Franklin chuckled. "Oh, don't make me laugh," he said. "It all hurts too much. What happened to me?"

Sheriff Thompson walked through the door to the room just at that moment.

"That's exactly what I'd like to know. What happened to you?" the sheriff said sourly.

Julie nodded at the sheriff as she moved to the other side of the bed, sitting in the visitor's chair there and taking Franklin's hand again.

Franklin was glad for the support as the sheriff continued to stand there staring down at him with his hard eyes.

"Well?" the sheriff said. "I'm waiting."

Franklin cleared his throat. "I came home from Darryl's last night. Late. About two-thirty in the morning. When I walked into my house, there was a man there."

"Describe him," the sheriff said, taking a notepad and pencil out of his sheriff's jacket pocket.

"He was a white man," Franklin said. "Little taller than me. Cold gray eyes. Was wearing blue scrubs, like what Julie wears sometimes."

The sheriff nodded, writing things down. "Go on."

"He was wearing a white mask, like a doctor's mask," Franklin added.

"A surgical mask?" Julie asked.

"Sure," Franklin said. He didn't know the name for them.

"Gloves?" Julie asked. "Like white surgical gloves?"

"Nope," Franklin said. "His hands was bare."

"What did he want?" the sheriff asked.

"An old knife of mine," Franklin said. "It were the oddest thing. He made sure I had my phone with me, told me to call 911, before he stabbed me."

"I looked at your report," Julie added. "You were stabbed in an area of the torso where there couldn't be much damage."

"So this guy was probably a doctor," the sheriff said.

"Or a nurse," Julie pointed out. "I'd know exactly where to stab a man to do both the most damage as well as the least."

After a moment of awkward silence, Franklin said, "That's my girl," as he squeezed her hand.

"Why did he want that knife?" the sheriff asked.

"Beats me," Franklin said. "But I think he was crazy. He talked about how the history books would remember me for it. How me and the knife were important."

The sheriff's eyebrows went up toward his hairline. "So what kind of knife was this?" he asked, continuing.

Franklin didn't see any reason to lie. "It was from her friend," he said, nodding toward Julie. "Eddie."

"The cra—I mean, the leader of the pagan cult we visited last year?" the sheriff asked.

"Yes. We mean to go down and talk with Eddie to see if she can tell us about the blade," Franklin added.

"Good luck with that," the sheriff said.

Franklin remembered that the sheriff had thought Eddie was useless the year before, when they'd been chasing the creature.

"Now tell me about your other wounds," the sheriff said. "The ones that look like they came from thorns."

"I was helping Darryl with a thorn bush out in his backyard," Franklin said, puzzled. Why did the sheriff want to know about those?

"The scratches and punctures were all infected. Just like the ones you got last year," the sheriff said dourly. "From that…whatever."

No wonder Franklin hurt so much.

"Now, I knew you was up to something," the sheriff added, pointing his pencil at Franklin. "You gonna tell me that thing is back?"

"No, sir," Franklin said. "It really was just a thorn bush in the back of Darryl's yard. Ornery critter, yes, but not about to come after anyone." He hoped.

"You sure about that?" the sheriff asked. "'Cause you really shouldn't be lying to me about that kind of thing. Even if I don't quite believe what happened."

"I'm sure," Franklin said. It had been an epic battle, but he was sure he'd won. Mostly.

After the sheriff had left, Julie gave Franklin a hard look. "Just a thorn bush?"

Franklin was glad he didn't have to lie to her. "Yes, ma'am. The blade was buried underneath it."

Julie was quiet for a moment. "It really has some power to it, don't it. This blade."

"'Fraid so."

"Then let's break you out of here. Get your scripts filled, and go down to see Eddie."

Franklin lay there thinking after Julie left to go badger the staff and the doctors. Eddie had refused her gift, would only sometimes let it move her.

But she was a good healer. She'd eased his soul the first time he'd seen her.

Somehow, he doubted she'd be able to do anything about the current pain in his side, the way it felt like the blade was still there.

Haunting him.

FRANKLIN ENJOYED the ride down to the next county to see Eddie. The sun had found its strength, being just after noon, though it weren't nearly as hot as the coming summer promised to be. Blue sky arched above them, going from horizon to horizon. Lots of green crops in the fields flew by, mostly sorghum and soy.

The last time Franklin had been so injured, it was mostly his back, from where the creature had picked him up then splatted him down on a bunch of broken glass. It had made sitting anywhere for any length of time painful.

This time, it was his sides that were aching—the left side, and shoulder, from where the bush had tagged him, and along his right, where the weight from the knife still held him down.

Julie had called ahead, but there hadn't been an answer. Eddie didn't believe in cell phones, and if she was out back in her shed, she wouldn't have heard the phone ring.

Still, Franklin was relieved when they drove up, a little past the house, and Julie pointed out the beat-up Jeep that belonged to Eddie, meaning that she was still there.

A tall wooden fence, painted white, ran from a corner of the house and blocked off the backyard from the street. Julie didn't bother knocking, just went through the gate as bold as brass.

Franklin knew that Eddie weren't the kind to keep guns to shoot trespassers, unlike Darryl. Still, he ducked his head and looked around the yard carefully before he stepped through.

The tall white fence went all the way around the yard, keeping out the prying eyes of the neighbors. Just in front of it grew a wild assortment of flowers, roses, and other bushes. The main house sat to the right, with what looked like a real nice screened-in porch facing the yard.

The shed sat to the left, under a large old oak tree. It weren't too big, smaller than a one-car garage. It had the look of an artist's studio, with red-painted wooden shingles covering the outer walls, white trim, and a gray tiled roof. Sweet incense oozed from it, floating over the bright spring grass.

"Eddie?" Julie called as she walked toward the studio. The door was closed this time, instead of a black curtain covering the opening.

Franklin hurried across the grass to join her.

As she was lifting her hand to knock on the door, it swung back. Eddie peered owlishly at them.

"Good morning," she said, though it was well past noon.

"I tried to call—" Julie said.

"No, no, I've been back here all day. I wouldn't have heard." She wiped her hands—covered in some kind of white material—down the front of her already white-smeared work apron. She looked the same as Franklin remembered her, a large, older white woman with tanned skin and wild white curls. Her blue eyes peered at them from atop a large nose, the kind good for sniffing out trouble. She had an easy smile, though, and looked happy to see them.

"Come on in," she said, stepping back into the studio. Workbenches lined three of the four walls, while a tall bookcase filled the fourth, its shelves lined with drying pottery, as well as a few books. Under the cloying sweet smell of incense lay the earthy scent of clay.

Most of the pottery pieces were little figures, like matching sets of suns and moons, horseshoes, and clusters of stars.

"Today's a day full of luck," Eddie explained as she walked over to the sink in the corner and washed her hands. "All these pieces will bring folks even more luck, particularly when made on a day like today."

Franklin had no idea if any of Eddie's work would actually bring a body luck. He also didn't think that was what her gift was, to make small figures. She should be working like Julie did, to cure folks, heal them.

However, he knew it weren't polite to say anything. Not that he ever would. He'd told her once that the spirits could move her more if she'd let them.

She'd claimed to be too old to learn new tricks.

"So how are you?" Eddie asked, stepping back from the sink and drying her hands. "I'm glad to see you. Both of you," she added, glancing at Franklin. Then she put her towel down and stood with her hands on her hips. "But I can tell this isn't a social call. You got something you need."

"Yes, ma'am," Julie said. She drew Franklin forward. "We need to know the history behind that blade of yours. The one you gave me last year. To help protect me from the creature."

Eddie shook her head. "There ain't much to tell, I'm afraid. I got the knife from an antique dealer in town."

Franklin sighed. He really hoped this wasn't going to be a wasted trip.

"Should we go talk with him?" Julie asked.

"Naw, fool didn't know what he had."

"What did he have, ma'am?" Franklin asked.

Eddie shrugged. "All I knew was that it was an object of power. So I took it before he could sell it to someone who might misuse it."

"Can you tell us anything else?" Julie asked. "Anything at all?"

"Well," Eddie started, then sighed. "I always kept that knife in a circle of protection. I didn't ever leave it out. The only folks who ever saw it were people from our group."

"Why did you keep it hidden?" Franklin asked. "What made you feel like you had to do that?"

"The knife was powerful," Eddie said. "When it was outside the circle, I felt sometimes like it was calling to me."

"And you just gave it to Julie? Without any instructions?"

Franklin asked. He wouldn't give in to his anger. But he also was never coming back here again. He'd be happier if Julie never came back either.

"I knew she'd give the knife to you," Eddie told him sharply. "And I knew that you'd be able to take care of it."

Franklin shook his head, bewildered. He hadn't known that he needed to do something more with that knife. He'd given it to Darryl for protection.

And look what had grown out of it.

"Thank you, ma'am," Franklin said, reaching for Julie's hand and tugging her back toward the door. "Y'all have a nice day."

They was halfway back across the yard before Eddie stuck her head out of her studio. "Wait," she said, following after them. "I'm sorry I can't help you. But I know someone who can."

Franklin waited, his patience just about run out.

"Her name's Beulah. She lives up at the end of Old Mill Road. You'll find the turnoff for it at the end of Main Street. She's…well, she's kind of odd. But I think she'll be able to tell you something about the knife. You've touched it recently, right?"

"Been stabbed with it," Franklin said dryly.

"Oh," Eddie said. "Then yes, go talk with Beulah. Tell her I sent you." Eddie paused, then looked squarely at Franklin. "May I?" she asked, reaching toward his injured side with her hands spread wide.

"Thank you, ma'am," Franklin said.

Eddie didn't actually touch him. He still felt the warmth from her palms radiating his skin.

Unfortunately, she didn't do much else. The wound still ached in a long, drawn-out way.

Either she wasn't following her own spirits and calling again.

Or the knife was much too strong.

Franklin didn't really want to know in either case.

∽

OLD MILL ROAD started off like a usual small town road, with ranch-style and other small houses stacked up on either side. Then the road left town and narrowed, going along fields, the brilliant green crops growing right up to the ditches running beside the road.

Once the road started climbing, it cooled off, leaving the clear open plains for woods. The road got rougher, until it weren't more than a dirt trail.

About a mile from where they left the highway were big "NO TRESPASSING" signs on either side of the road, that were then repeated less than a quarter mile away.

One even had a red skull and crossbones on it, with the words, "Trespassers will be violated."

Franklin didn't much like the looks of that at all.

But he'd done his fair share of talking with hicks and hillbillies. He figured this Beulah wouldn't be crazier than anyone he'd already met. Probably not any worse than most of the folks who made up his own family.

The road dead ended just a bit further up. A wooden cabin—more like a shack—lurked on the left side. Moss covered the roof, and lichen and vines grew up the sides. Trees hunched nearby. An old over-stuffed chair, stained with bird droppings and black moss, sat on one side of the single door. A gray blanket covered the window.

"Well, here goes nothing," Julie said. She reached over and squeezed Franklin's hand.

"I don't know about that," Franklin said sourly. "That sure looks like something."

But he weren't about to back down. He got out of the car and took Julie's hand before they walked closer to the house.

"Stop right there," came a gruff voice.

A woman came barreling out of the house.

Franklin took it as a good sign that she didn't have a shotgun pointed right at them.

She was, however, shaking an evil-looking wand at them, about three feet long. The tip of it held a blue stone, shaped like an arrowhead. Sharp metal spikes stuck out on all sides just below it. Bones dangled just below that, long ones, like ribs and forearm bones. In between them hung ratty ribbons that might have once been white.

The woman holding the wand looked like a Hollywood version of a hillbilly, right down to the one large snaggletooth in the front of her mouth with the one beside it missing. She was a large woman, not white or black, but mixed. She had brown eyes that stared out from a broad face, her nose melting across it like something had scared it out of growing tall. A colorful red bandana held back black dreadlocks. She wore a stained, green-and-white flannel shirt over a pair of ratty gray sweatpants.

"Beulah?" Franklin asked, stepping forward, slightly in front of Julie. "My name's Franklin. Franklin Kanly. This here's Julie Horton. Eddie sent us." It weren't that he believed that Beulah could do anything with that wand.

He weren't about to take a chance, though.

Beulah sniffed, unimpressed. "What's that poser want?" she asked, not lowering the wand but centering it instead right over Franklin's heart.

It was probably just his imagination—or his paranoia—that the center of his chest suddenly felt warm.

"Ma'am, did you ever…meet that blade of Eddie's?" Franklin asked. He couldn't imagine Beulah coming down out of the hills to go meet with someone like Eddie, couldn't see her in Eddie's artist's studio.

Eddie wouldn't allow a dirty hillbilly like Beulah into her clean house.

Beulah tilted her head to one side. "Funny you ask that. Had another man—a white man—come up and ask about that same knife not more than a month ago."

"Really?" Franklin asked. He stopped himself from taking another step forward, as Beulah's wand continued to heat up his chest. "Can you tell me what he looked like?"

"Why should I tell you anything at all?" Beulah asked.

It was a fair question. Franklin didn't want to be spreading his troubles around, but he had to gain this woman's trust.

"Because someone—possibly this man—stabbed me with that blade," Franklin said.

Beulah's wand seemed to move of its own accord, directing her hand unerringly to the right side where Franklin had been injured.

"I see," Beulah said. She abruptly raised her wand back up, holding it upright and to the side, like an ancient knight might have held a sword. "I can't tell you much of anything about him. He was a white man, older. Head shaved, but white fringe all along the edges. Talked snooty. Offered me a lot of money for what I could tell him."

Julie tugged on Franklin's hand so he looked over at her. She raised her eyebrows in question.

"Yeah, that sounds like him," Franklin said. "So can you tell us anything about that blade?"

Beulah gave him a great, large grin, showing off more rotten and missing teeth between her thin lips. "I can," she said. "But you ain't gonna like it."

Franklin nodded grimly. He already knew there weren't nothing about this day for him to like.

THE INSIDE of Beulah's cabin smelled of fresh cedar and rosemary. It was dim after the bright spring sunlight outside, and seemed crowded with magazines stacked everywhere, a loveseat encased in a stained floral cover sagging just right of the door, broken wooden straight-back chairs piled in the far corner. At least the wooden floor had been swept clean.

Bunches of rosemary, dill, sage, and thyme hung from the rafters, drying, along with strands of garlic. A huge wood-burning stove took up most of the left wall, and an oversized wooden rocking chair, topped with stained cushions and pillows, sat in front of it.

Beulah stopped just inside the door, then turned and pointed to Franklin's and Julie's feet. "Shoes," she commanded.

Franklin nodded, surprised, but he complied, slipping his sneakers off.

It would make leaving in a hurry more difficult, but he weren't about to question how a woman wanted to keep her house.

"This way," Beulah said, leading them through the dim living room and into the kitchen.

There, sunlight streamed through the back windows. The walls were covered in clean white tiles, laid like bricks. Green linoleum covered the floor, carefully repaired with duct tape and flooring samples that didn't match where it had cracked. Two stoves took up the near wall—one a modern, electric edition, the other, an ancient, black iron wood-burning version.

A long skinny harvest table took up the center of the room. It had a reddish hue to it, that Franklin assumed came from the cherry wood and not from chickens he heard clucking in a coop out back. More herbs hung from the ceiling here, filling the room with cooking smells, like oregano and sage.

"I need you to lay down here," Beulah said, indicating the table. "And hike your shirt up."

"Why?" Franklin asked. Why did she want him to bare himself? They were just here for information.

"I don't know anything about that blade," Beulah said adamantly.

Franklin looked at Julie. How far was it to the door?

"But I *can* find out the history of it," Beulah bragged.

"How?" Franklin asked. Was this what Eddie meant, by how Beulah could help them? That she'd be able to *find* the history of it?

"It stabbed you here, right?" Beulah asked, her wand suddenly pointing toward his side again.

Franklin tried to control his flinch. "Yes, ma'am."

"I need to draw some blood. Just a little," she added quickly. "Then use that to conjure the blade's past."

Franklin didn't like this. Not one bit.

"How will you draw the blood?" Julie asked, professional.

That at least made Franklin feel better. Julie would make sure it was done right.

"What, you a nurse or something?" Beulah asked, challenging.

"I am," Julie said. She fished her hospital ID out of her purse and showed it to Beulah.

Did Beulah know her letters? She appeared to, mouthing the name of Julie's hospital silently.

Beulah gave Julie a hard look up and down, moving her wand in small circles close to Julie's chest. "Huh," was all she said after a moment.

Then she turned, opened a drawer, and pulled out a black knife that appeared to be made of stone. "I was planning on using this."

"Ooooh," Julie said. She touched the blade gingerly. "That will do."

"What is that?" Franklin asked. He figured he had a right to know, since they was planning on using it to slice him open, get at his blood.

"It's an obsidian blade," Julie explained.

"A what?" Franklin asked.

"Obsidian is a type of volcanic glass," Julie explained. "There's been some studies done with surgery blades being made out of obsidian. The actual edge of the blade is finer and sharper than most metal blades because it's only microns wide."

"Okay," Franklin said slowly, not sure he understood all of that.

"It's safer and better to be cut by that blade than by most," Julie assured him.

"I trust you," Franklin said.

As soon as the words was out of his mouth he realized that meant them, and not in a casual way. But rather, in a deeper, heartfelt way. He caught her gaze and held it for a moment, trying to express what he meant, what he was feeling.

Julie smiled at him and reached out, squeezing his arm briefly.

"If y'all is done," Beulah said dryly.

"Sorry, ma'am," Franklin said. "What do you need?"

"Shirt off," Beulah instructed.

Franklin turned his back on the two women and slipped his T-shirt off over his head, feeling oddly exposed.

He knew that his cousin Darryl would be cheering him on, right now, telling him that this was how all the best porn movies started.

Franklin had watched some of that porn. He hadn't thought it was any good at all.

When Franklin turned back around, he was surprised that Beulah didn't focus immediately on his side.

"What the hell else you been doing?" she asked, holding her hand up, a few inches from his bandaged shoulder, where the thorn had bit him.

"Fighting with a thorn bush," Franklin said. "The one that grew up over where that blade was buried."

Beulah's eyebrows rose up toward her hairline but she didn't say anything. Instead, she gestured for Franklin to lay down on the table.

Julie gently pried loose the dressing over Franklin's injured side. At least the wound there had only required stitches. It weren't all red and angry like the thorn punctures.

While Beulah got a large pot for her stove, filled it with water, and started stirring herbs into it, chanting nonsense syllables, Julie took Franklin's hand and squeezed it. "You doin' okay?" she asked.

Franklin looked up at her. "I'm doing fine."

Julie winked at him. "Look fine too," she whispered.

Franklin was again glad that his blush couldn't be seen because of his dark skin. He hadn't been keeping up with his weekly workouts with his Ab-Buster. But he had been doing more physical work, hauling crates of produce at the stand, as well as more pushups, at Karl's suggestion. They'd even put up an iron bar, out back, so they could do pullups. Franklin was getting better at those, too.

Finally, Beulah was ready. She prayed over the blade, some words in English, some words in a language that Franklin didn't understand, but that sounded soft and slurred together. Julie nodded along now and again—he'd have to ask her about it, later.

With a quick flick of her wrist, Beulah cut along Franklin's skin right above where the stitches for the knife were. The cut wasn't deep, and didn't sting until after she was finished.

Julie had been right, though. It barely bled.

With an overhand, extravagant wave of her arm, Beulah flicked the drops of blood gathered on the blade into the pot of water on her electric stove.

Steam instantly boiled up and flowed over the edges, like a witch's cauldron.

Franklin couldn't help but shiver.

The steam didn't contain images, not that Franklin could see.

But he could recognize its power.

This steam reminded him of the regular ghosts who sought him out—something that was between one place and the next. Maybe between the here and now and the past.

Fascinated, Franklin sat up to stare harder at the pot. Beulah was still chanting, swaying and moving her hips more gracefully than he would have thought possible. She danced in time with a music he didn't quite hear, but he knew it came from the steam and her cauldron.

There was something there. In that mist. He could tell.

He just couldn't see it. Not like she could.

Beulah started to moan.

The sound sent more shivers down Franklin's back. Julie silently handed him his shirt, and Franklin gratefully slipped it back on.

Then Julie sat beside him on the table and they waited with dread while Beulah finished her reading.

Franklin wasn't about to turn back now, but he wasn't looking forward to whatever it was that Beulah had to say.

CHAPTER 6

"You know what you get when you cross a spider with a snake and a bat?" Beulah asked.

Franklin shook his head. It sounded like the start of a joke that he didn't know, the kind Darryl would tell.

Franklin and Julie sat out in the backyard of Beulah's shack, perched on the remains of stumps carefully placed around a great bonfire pit. The sun peeked over the surrounding trees. Birds sang wildly just beyond the edge of the trees, while the cicadas cycled up and down. The woods smelled of mulch and green things, freshly growing.

Next to the house was a well-kept coop for the chickens, with a pen for the birds to scratch in. They'd gone back to quietly clucking to themselves once they'd realized no feed was coming.

It reminded Franklin of Lexine's cabin, though she had more garden in her backyard. She also took care of her place more. However, this was Beulah's…focus spot, for want of a better term. Franklin would bet that she spent a lot of time with the bonfire going, feeding the flames and reading the smoke.

"That blade weren't merely forged. It were conjured, constructed to take lives—souls—and suck them free of a body," Beulah said. She paced in front of Franklin and Julie, from one side of the bonfire pit to the other.

Franklin shivered in the bright daylight. "So the knife's evil," he said.

"No, it ain't," Beulah said. "Weren't no demons or otherworldly creatures involved. All natural."

"But you said it takes souls," Franklin protested.

"Taking a soul don't make it evil," Beulah interrupted. "Y'all have raised chickens, right?"

Franklin nodded. He hadn't, actually, raised chickens. Though he liked eggs well enough, it was just him, and the stupid birds weren't worth the bother.

But he had slaughtered Sweet Bess, the hog he'd raised. She'd been much more like a dog than a pig. A big, nasty, *mean* dog, but still. So he understood what Beulah was getting at.

"It's what you *do* with the soul afterward that makes it good or bad," Beulah explained. "It were originally created for sacrifices. A way of honoring their gods."

"Their gods?" Franklin asked. It didn't surprise him too much that it was a foreign knife.

"There's more out there than just your white-bearded old man," Beulah warned.

Julie squeezed Franklin's hand in warning when he would have spoken up.

Instead, he nodded, keeping his words to himself. "So it weren't created to do evil," he clarified. "But it weren't created to do good, either."

Beulah shrugged. "It could do good," she said. "In the right hand."

Franklin pressed his lips together and didn't say anything, though he didn't see how taking souls could ever be a good thing.

"The blade's history is cloudy after its maker was slaughtered," Beulah said. "It wasn't being used much, and when it was used, it wasn't being used right. It wasn't doing what it was created to do."

She paused, then fixed Franklin with a hard stare. "It woke up when it was in your hand," she told Franklin. "Wanting to take the souls of those ghosts of yours."

Franklin gulped. He remembered sitting at the kitchen table, holding the blade, threatening the ghosts of Mama and Gloria. It weren't his proudest moment.

"So what would it do with those souls?" Franklin asked after a moment.

"What would you want for it to do with them?" Beulah countered.

"Send them Beyond," Franklin said. "Help them pass through." When Beulah looked at him, puzzled, Franklin added, "Ghosts get stuck sometimes."

Beulah smiled like a cat who'd just gotten into the cream. "Ghosts, eh?" she asked.

Franklin felt his back stiffen. "Yes, ma'am." He weren't about to deny it.

"Would what you be doing with the knife be evil?" Beulah asked.

"No, ma'am," Franklin said firmly. "But it would be cheatin'. To just send 'em on. Not let 'em work out what they needed to do before they left."

Beulah gave Julie a huge grin at that. "He's a keeper," she commented casually.

"Yes, ma'am, he is," Julie said, squeezing his hand.

Even though the women couldn't see him blush, Franklin suspected that neither woman needed to see his skin turn red to know what it was he was feeling.

"So the blade was meant to take souls," Franklin said, trying to get the conversation back on track. "What is the doctor gonna do with it?"

"Doctor?" Beulah asked.

"The man who stabbed me with the knife. He was wearing doctor clothes," Franklin explained. "Scrubs."

"Doctors generally heal people," Beulah said.

"They can also kill," Julie added quietly. "Like the ones who decide that someone has suffered enough. Help them on."

"Angel of mercy," Beulah said. "Could see that."

"Is that really evil?" Franklin asked. He wouldn't have wanted Mama to suffer after her heart attack, if it hadn't killed her outright.

Beulah cocked her head to one side. "What you do with your ghosts isn't evil. But using the knife, you said it would be cheating. That doctor of yours, he's looking for a cheat. A shortcut. To something."

"To what?"

"Power."

FRANKLIN WALKED out the front door of Beulah's shack with Julie in front of him. As she walked to the car, Beulah wrapped one of her meaty hands around Franklin's arm, stopping him.

"You know, that blade liked you," she said.

Up close, Beulah smelled of dirt and not enough baths, her breath foul with rot.

But he didn't try to get away, despite how uncomfortable he was with anyone touching him. Instead, he shrugged.

He didn't feel the same way about the blade.

"It's still connected to you," Beulah added.

"What do you mean?" Franklin asked, alarmed.

Beulah paused. "Don't know rightly how to explain it. But it left a part of itself—a ghost, maybe—inside you. When you was stabbed."

Franklin shivered. He didn't like the sound of that at all. Though that was exactly how it felt.

Julie was at the side of the car door and had turned back, realizing that Franklin wasn't behind her. He raised his hand, reassuring her that he was okay, that she should stay there.

"It was why I was able to give you so many details about its history," Beulah said. "Normally, I gots to touch something to know so much about it. But it's in your blood."

"Thank you, ma'am," Franklin said when Beulah didn't have anything more to add. He tugged his arm gently free.

"I ever have any ghost problems, I'm sending them to you," Beulah added as Franklin crossed back to the car.

Franklin nodded. That was only fair. Though he'd also given Beulah most of the money in his wallet for the reading.

As they backed out of the clearing, Julie asked, "You okay?"

Franklin sighed, but decided he needed to keep telling Julie the truth. "That knife wound? It's never felt right." He didn't tell her it still felt as though the blade was in his side—that Beulah had just told him it might be.

Julie nodded, reaching over and squeezing his knee. "Let me know how I can help."

Franklin didn't have a clue. Maybe he could go visit Preacher Sinclair. Have him pray the ghost of the blade out of his side.

Though, somehow, he doubted that would be enough.

FRANKLIN PUZZLED and puzzled all through dinner about what the doctor (since that seemed to be what they was now calling the man who'd stabbed him) wanted to do with that blade, that soul stealer.

They'd stopped at a roadside diner, one that promised authentic home cooking and heavenly pies. It fit with Franklin's idea of a diner, with red vinyl booth seats, a cracked linoleum floor, and pictures of the local baseball team—going back decades—pasted all around the cash register.

The waitress who'd served them was probably barely out of high school and pregnant. At least she looked happy about it, snapping her gum as she took their order, coming back often to see how they was doing.

The chicken-fried steak wasn't as good as Mama's—nothing would ever top that. But it was a close second, and the mashed potatoes was perfect, with just the right amount of whip and butter in them to make them fluffy.

Still, Franklin couldn't pay as much attention to the food as it deserved, his mind too preoccupied.

Finally, after the dinner plates had been removed and they was waiting on pie, he asked Julie, "Have you figured out what the doctor wanted with that blade?"

Julie shook her head. "You said it took a lot of energy to conjure your mama up."

"It did," Franklin said. "It must have taken a lot from him to bring back those other two ghosts too. But why did he do it?"

"Well, by bringing them back, he was able to make you go and get that blade," Julie pointed out.

Franklin gave a low whistle. "He's smart. Came up with the only thing that would make me dig it up."

"Why do you think he didn't try to dig it up himself?" Julie asked.

Franklin snorted. "That thorn bush weren't tame. It took a lot to defeat it. Plus, Darryl would have shot anyone he thought was trespassing in his backyard. No, he had to wait until I got it."

"You could ask Georgia if he came snooping around the house any," Julie pointed out.

"Not sure what good that would do," Franklin said. "He already has the blade. The question is what's he gonna do with it?"

"If he raises more of the dead, brings back ghosts, could he take their souls?" Julie asked.

"That's what I was thinking," Franklin said. He smiled at Julie.

Normally, Franklin didn't believe in touching in public. Particularly not a nice white woman like Julie, particularly not a new place he'd never been at before. In a town like this.

But he really wanted to take her hand across the table. He tried, instead, to show her how he felt about her with his eyes, how much he admired how smart she was. "So he raises ghosts back up, brings them out of their well-earned rest—or rips them out of Heaven—and then...does what with them?"

"I don't know," Julie said. "With the blade, he could then take their souls and use them, somehow."

"Got to be something big, though," Franklin said. "If it takes so much out of him to raise them in the first place. It's gotta be something big. Some kind of big magic or spell."

Franklin felt distinctly uncomfortable with those words coming out of his mouth. He didn't cast spells or dabble in magic. He just did his duty, helping ghosts along.

This doctor, though, he did something more like what a witch would do.

"If he is a doctor, or was, then he might be trying to heal someone," Julie said.

"Or some*thing*," Franklin pointed out. "Like a wound in the earth." Just healing a single person wouldn't take that much effort. Not if the doctor could raise the dead.

Just then, their pies arrived. Franklin's still steamed from being fried on the grill, the vanilla ice cream melting perfectly beside it.

It sure looked heavenly.

And so did Julie, sitting across from him. Even if he couldn't take her hand. It was as close to perfect as he was likely to get in this world.

Something even that blade couldn't cut through.

FULL AND SATISFIED, Franklin let out a small belch as they was driving home.

"Sorry. Excuse me," he said, apologizing to Julie, not feeling sorry, not one bit. He was too damned content to feel bad.

Julie just grinned at him. "That was mighty good."

"It sure was," Franklin said. While Franklin loved cooking with Julie on their nights in, he also enjoyed going out with her.

Feeling daring, he reached across the divide between them and lightly touched her thigh.

Julie dropped one hand down from the steering wheel and wrapped it around his.

Though Franklin was still injured, and Julie was a nurse and a stickler for taking it easy, maybe they could still spend some time making out on the sofa that night.

Suddenly, the pain in Franklin's right side spiked hard, where the knife had been plunged into him. He couldn't help but twitch, abruptly squeezing Julie's thigh hard.

"Sorry," he said, removing his hand. Then he gasped as the next wave of pain hit.

"Franklin?" Julie asked, worried. "What's goin' on?"

"The knife," Franklin gasped. The pain intensified, a single steel point of lava burning in his side.

As quickly as it had come, the pain left, leaving Franklin panting.

Julie had already pulled over to the shoulder of the highway. She had one hand on his forehead. "You're burning up," she murmured. "Infection?"

"No," Franklin said, grabbing onto her wrist when she would have pulled away. "At least, that's not what I think it is." He took a couple of deep breaths, trying to sort out what was going on.

The knife—no, the blade—was in pain.

"The doctor's doing something to the blade," Franklin finally got out. "It has three prongs on it, right?"

"Yes," Julie said, still worried.

"The doctor...oh, jeez...the doctor is shaving away one of them," Franklin ground out.

"How do you know?" Julie asked, worried.

"The blade's calling out to me," Franklin told her. "It's still connected to me. Like it left something inside me. When the doctor stabbed me with it."

Julie frowned at him. "Have you been feeling that since the start?" she asked.

"Yes, ma'am," Franklin said. "I didn't want to tell you, though. I didn't want to worry you."

Even in the dim light, Julie's glare was strong enough to make Franklin wince again, and not from the pain in his side.

"You need to tell me that kind of thing," Julie said. "You got to share. Or we're never gonna make it. Not long term."

Franklin blinked. He knew that he wanted for them to make it, for them to keep being a couple. For them to maybe, someday, live together out at his farm.

Maybe even get married.

He'd never assumed that Julie might want the same things, though.

"Really?" he asked, his voice soft with wonder. "You want to make it long term? With me?"

Julie rolled her eyes at him. "Of course I do. Idiot."

Franklin wondered about telling your partner things that were important, like being with them long term, but he didn't say nothing.

Then the pain washed over him again, stealing his breath away and making the world dim.

"Franklin? Honey?" Julie's voice sounded very far away.

From behind Franklin's shut eyes he could see a gray line, leading across the fields, leading straight to where the blade was suffering.

"That way," he rasped, pointing a finger. "We got to go that way."

He felt Julie's lips brush against his forehead. "You just keep telling me the direction. I ain't gonna cross country in my car unless I have to. I have to keep taking roads."

Franklin nodded, then said, "Okay."

The call of the blade was strong.

But so was Julie's hand, resting on his thigh, keeping him present.

Between them, it was gonna be okay.

THEY KEPT DRIVING MOSTLY north and then east, in turns. The night sky was clear, the stars distant points of light that Franklin could barely see, the sky washed out by the highway lights. Only a few other cars traveled with them along the road, mainly semis and other professional drivers.

When Franklin saw an exit for Perrysville, he felt a stronger twinge. "There," he said, pointing it out to Julie.

The pain had gotten worse. Franklin wasn't sure he'd be able to stand once they got to where ever it was they was going. But he'd do whatever it was that needed doing.

In a way, this was like his duty, too. Stopping this doctor from hurting other ghosts, disrupting the natural flow of things.

He really didn't like dragging Julie into the middle of this, though. He'd never forgive himself if she got hurt.

Then again, he weren't sure he could stop her, not at this point.

And there was a very small voice inside of him that didn't want to, that was glad she'd come along for the ride.

Perryville was a typical tourist town, with a couple of large hotels on the outskirts of town and lots of historic buildings inside the city limits, with plenty of plaques for people to read all about the events that had happened there.

But the blade weren't in the town, not in any of the buildings. Instead, Franklin directed them through the town, past the old Civil War museum, then out again.

On the road to the Perryville Battlefield.

Big signs on either side of the entrance to the State Park declared the park closed.

If the doctor was ignoring those, so could they.

Julie slowed down some, creeping up the lane toward the Civil War memorial.

They approached a big sign giving information about the battle at Perryville. "Stop here, please," Franklin said.

Julie obliged.

Franklin rolled down his window and stuck his head out, reading the sign. Then he sat back, worried. "Says over seven thousand soldiers died during the battle of Perryville."

"Seven thousand?" Julie asked. "That's a lot of souls."

Franklin nodded. Were all those soldiers buried here? Would it matter to the ghosts? Could they be raised where they died? Mama had had her heart attack in the kitchen. Was that why the doctor could raise her there?

Franklin had never dealt with old souls before. All the ghosts he saw were modern-day people, who'd died recently and couldn't pass on.

What would an old ghost be like? Raised from over a century ago? Would it be stronger? More angry?

And what was the doctor going to do with all those souls?

"You don't have to go with me," Franklin told Julie as they parked in the lot behind the museum.

"Now you see? That's where you're wrong," Julie told Franklin firmly as she got out of the car.

Franklin followed suit, though he just stood on his side, struggling to breathe through the pain.

Julie hurried over to where he was standing, looking at him critically. "You're bleeding," she said flatly.

Franklin looked down. It weren't much blood, just a bit through the bandage on his side. "I been resting it," he complained.

"Not sure that matters," Julie said, obviously worried. "Now, come on. We got an insane doctor to stop."

Franklin took her hand and paused, just for a moment, wanting to kiss her.

He knew he shouldn't. But there weren't no one there to see. And he didn't know when the next time would be that it would be safe to kiss her.

So he leaned down and kissed her lightly anyway. "Thank you," he whispered against her lips.

"For what?" Julie asked.

"For everything," Franklin said.

"You're welcome. Now let's go stop a madman."

Franklin nodded and fell into step beside her.

While he wanted to stop the doctor, and he knew that it was important, he was also aware that protecting his love had a much higher priority than ever before.

THEY WALKED along the walkway through the open field, passing by signs of interest, explaining the battle and the farm it had been fought on. It was a bit chilly, so Franklin gave his jacket to Julie, over her protests that he'd been wounded and needed it instead.

Franklin wished they was taking this walk for some other reason, that they weren't so desperate and scared. At least the pain in his side had diminished.

Whatever the doctor had done to the blade, however much he'd shaved off of it, he was finished.

For now.

Franklin still felt the blade calling to him. As they reached a grassy hill he turned, abruptly, tugging at Julie's hand. "This way," he said.

The hill gently sloped down to a narrow valley, then up again. Mist gathered in long lines across the bottom of the hill. An old cannon on a cement block pointed toward the sky. There weren't any cover on the slope, no trees to hide behind, no rocks either. Franklin felt exposed standing there, as if that old cannon could suddenly turn and fire on them.

But the blade was calling to him, just up the next hill.

The cicada chorus suddenly dimmed and the night grew still, as if it were holding its breath.

More mist rose out of the grassy slope. Could they hide in that if it grew thick enough? Franklin started leading Julie that way, straight down the hill, then stopped abruptly when the mist split itself, dividing into separate pieces.

Separate bodies.

Ghosts.

Franklin had never seen so many ghosts all in one place before. He'd only ever dealt with one or two at a time.

The cold they gave off spiked through his bones, making him shiver.

These weren't regular ghosts, either. They was the raised ones, with holes for eyes and a despair blacker than the night. No *intent*, nothing they needed doing, just rage.

Old, *old* rage boiled out of them, anger about the war and dying too young and now being ripped out of what little peace they'd found.

Some of them wore uniforms that Franklin recognized from watching documentaries on TV.

"Can you see those?" Franklin whispered to Julie, pulling up short.

"See what?" Julie asked, also whispering.

"Nothing," Franklin said, relieved.

"Nope. I don't see nothing. Except the armies of ghosts in front of us," Julie added. She thwapped him on his shoulder, expertly missing all his existing injuries. "What did I say about sharing these things with me?"

"Sorry," Franklin said. And he was. He vowed to do better. "These aren't regular ghosts, you know," he whispered. "These are the raised ones."

Julie nodded. "They aren't really *there*, are they? They keep shifting, fading out."

Franklin nodded. He would bet that the only reason Julie was seeing anything was because he was still holding her hand. If it got too bad, he could always let go, though she'd probably yell at him for that.

But he also understood what she meant. The doctor was raising lines of ghosts, one at a time, in a wave. A line of ghosts would rise up, then the next, then the next, and the first line would start to fade.

"Why is he raising all these ghosts? How is he doing it?" Julie asked.

"The blade," Franklin said, suddenly understanding. "He was shaving off part of the blade before. He's using its power to raise these souls, draw them to him." Cheating, again.

But why?

The doctor had to be at the top of the hill in front of them. They was gonna have to skirt around the valley, see if they could get closer without being seen.

A single crop of trees stood on the south slope of the hill, close to the top. It would hide them from view if they climbed from that side, maybe until they could rush out and surprise the doctor.

"This way," Franklin told Julie, tugging on her hand.

"Why don't we just go across the valley and up the hill?" Julie asked, not moving. "I don't think he's gonna hurt us none. And we could ruin his—"

The first of the ghosts stated howling.

The sound turned Franklin's insides to jelly. Now, Franklin had never thought of himself as a brave man. Sure, he'd faced a lot of ghosts, but that was just doing his duty.

This howling came straight from Hell. It made him shiver all the way to his bones. It was the most awful sound he'd ever heard. Angry and terrifying, like demons was chasing the ghosts, on their tail and they couldn't escape, there weren't any way out.

If they'd been in Heaven before, now they was in Hell. And they didn't like it, not one bit. Like God himself had turned his back on them.

Julie's eyes grew big. She opened her mouth, then shut it again. "Around. We go around." She looked at the ghosts gathered below them and shivered.

Franklin nodded. But before he started walking again, he held up their linked hands. "If I let go, you might not hear that noise as much," he told her, offering her the choice instead of just letting go. "Might not see as much either."

He figured she'd prefer the choice, rather than him just letting go, trying to protect her.

Julie thought for a moment, then squeezed his hand tighter. "Don't even think about it," she whispered fiercely. "We're in this together."

Franklin couldn't tell Julie that he loved her. It weren't the right time, on a battlefield with an army of ghosts from Hell howling below them. She might not think it was real.

But Franklin knew, suddenly, that this was it. What he was feeling was real.

They just had to survive the rest of the night so he could tell her proper.

CHAPTER 7

THE HOWLING of the ghosts got louder as Franklin and Julie skirted the hill. Seemed that the doctor was raising ghosts in a circle, on all sides of the hill he were standing on.

Was he staying up there so he had a better view of everything? Or did he have some kind of protection up there, so the ghosts couldn't get at him? Would they have something more to fight once they got closer?

Franklin thought it had to be for protection. Those ghosts were *angry*. He'd bet they'd give Mama a run for the money in glaring power, even if their eyes was hollowed out. He weren't sure what they could do to the living—besides scare 'em to death—but there was so many ghosts. Maybe they could combine and have more power to move things.

At least they weren't trying to get in Franklin's way as he hurried to the side of the hill.

Franklin had walked into his share of ghosts, or had them walk through him. The worst thing about that kind of happenstance was the cold, freezing him worse than ice slipped down his back.

But so many ghosts all in one place generated their own type of cold. Instead of spiking through Franklin, it was like a living thing, creeping over his skin and coating it in a blanket of ice.

Suddenly, the ground underneath their feet trembled.

Franklin didn't like that one bit.

"What's he doing?" Franklin asked as he rushed them around another clump of ghosts.

"Don't know," Julie said.

Franklin stopped and looked at Julie. Her teeth were chattering, and Franklin had never seen her look so pale.

Or scared.

She held up her free hand before he could say anything. "Don't even think about suggesting we turn back. We've got to stop this doctor. What he's doing is *wrong.*"

Franklin meekly nodded. "Would it help if you closed your eyes?" he asked. The ghosts around them loomed closer. "I can lead us up the hill."

Julie shut her eyes briefly, then snapped them open again. "Nope. But thanks. Let's just get going."

Franklin tucked Julie's hand closer, under his arm, trying to warm it up. She was freezing, despite wearing is jacket. At least she was wearing jeans and not her usual shorts.

A lone clump of pine trees huddled together near the top of the hill. Just beyond them, a sickly yellow light glowed.

Franklin recognized that light. It looked like what the doctor had used to raise Mama.

Only this light was much bigger, spreading out like mist, creeping along the ground.

Franklin led Julie into the trees, the sweet smell of pine surrounding them. The brown needles under the trees muffled their footsteps.

At least there weren't any ghosts there.

The trees started swaying as they hurried underneath them.

Franklin didn't realize his mistake until they was almost to the edge.

He remembered Miss Adrianna, how her trees reached down with their branches, holding her hand, like they was her children.

These trees had also been woken up.

But like the ghosts, they was angry.

Hard branches grabbed at Franklin's arms. Harsh needles stung his skin. "Ow!" Franklin complained, though he tried to keep his voice hushed. His shoulder still ached from where the thorn bush had bit him, the stitches in his side pulling, sharp and tight.

The branches immediately loosened their grip. However, they didn't let go—neither Franklin nor Julie would be allowed to pass.

The trees weren't trying to hurt them either.

Franklin turned to see Julie. She was just as stuck as he was, held tight.

Were the trees trying to protect them? Or was they protecting the doctor? Franklin didn't know. He tugged at the branches holding onto his arms, but he couldn't get himself loose.

Just beyond the trees, Franklin thought he saw a solitary ghost. His uniform was torn and muddy, and the bandage around his head looked like it still bled.

Like the other ghosts, his eyes was dark and hollow. But he moved apart from the others, as though he'd held onto some of his will. He appeared to nod at Franklin, then ambled back down the hill, disappearing.

Franklin turned back forward. The doctor continued his spell. He had a camp table set up with a gas lantern on it, the old-fashioned kind that burned kerosene. The blade lay on one side, whimpering. Instead of three, equal-sized edges running the length of it, one had been shaved away.

Franklin didn't know what was in that witch's cauldron bubbling in the center of the table, that had the sickly yellow mist pouring out of it, but he'd bet the pieces of the blade were there.

The doctor was in his familiar scrubs, but he weren't wearing a mask. Maybe he didn't expect to be caught this time. Franklin studied his face, trying to memorize it, so if Sheriff Thompson asked maybe he could describe it to a sketch artist, like they did on TV.

The doctor had a strong jaw. It seemed to stick out from the rest of his face as he chanted in that weird language he'd used before, twisting his tongue and chewing on the words. His nose was just a tiny thing compared to the rest of his face, short and flat, while his forehead pushed out over his beady eyes.

He was older than Franklin would have guessed, probably in his late fifties or early sixties. His scalp was mostly bare, with just white fringes around the edges, curly.

This had to be the same man who'd gone to see Beulah. Who'd stabbed Franklin.

But why was he raising an army of ghosts? What was his *intent?*

Franklin could only wait and watch.

~

WHEN THE GROUND RUMBLED AGAIN, Franklin looked around, trying to see what the hell it was.

The ghosts of cannonballs flew through the air, raising from the valley up to the top of the hill.

Was the doctor gonna fight a war? Or was that the ghosts, trying to fight back?

But the cannonballs didn't strike the doctor, or his table. They pounded the hill, causing the ground to shake.

Franklin sure was glad he'd never had to go to war. What little he was seeing was awful.

The howls of the dead grew louder, drowning out all the other sounds. Franklin weren't sure if he called out to Julie if she'd hear him. She looked pale hanging there.

Franklin tried breaking himself free again, but he couldn't get to her.

At least he weren't holding her hand anymore. Maybe the screams weren't as loud for her, piercing her soul, though from her face was crunched up together, he knew some of the terrible racket were getting through.

Finally, the doctor finished with his spell. The howls of the dead died down to just moaning on the wind, constantly sending chills down Franklin's spine.

Franklin looked over to where Julie hung, also trapped in the trees. She was watching the doctor too. She glanced over at Franklin and said something.

Franklin couldn't quite catch it, but if he was reading her lips right, she'd just said, "I know him."

Julie knew the doctor? Had she worked with him? Did she still work with him?

"My brave soldiers!" the doctor called out, addressing the army of the dead before him.

The ghosts howled in reply.

"I know you bravely gave your lives once in the defense of this country," the doctor continued once they died down. "Blue or gray, it doesn't matter. However, I ask for your lives once again, in the service of our great people."

The ghosts howled again, louder this time. Franklin felt himself trying to back away, though the trees held him fast.

It weren't right, whatever the hell this doctor were about to do. And Franklin wanted no part of it.

"No death! No birth! Just life eternal!" the doctor called out.

What the hell did that mean?

The doctor held up the blade, though it weren't happy with him, not one bit.

If the blade had any ability to move, it would have driven itself into the doctor, tried its darnedest to take his soul. Bite him.

But the blade was just a tool, and the doctor was much more powerful than it was.

The ghosts surged up the hill, so many bodies that they hid Franklin's view of the doctor. The cold rolled out from them, making Franklin's teeth chatter.

Then they started to thin. The wide river of ghosts became a stream, all flowing toward the doctor and the blade he had raised over his head.

What was the doctor doing? Why had he raised so many souls, just to take them again?

The blade started complaining. It weren't made to take and hold so many souls, not all at once.

Suddenly, instead of everything rolling *in*, it all rolled *out*, like a mighty belch that the doctor couldn't quite contain.

Heat blasted Franklin, baking his front. It was like suddenly stepping close to a camping fire. The warmth sunk deep into his skin, seeping into his bones.

The trees sighed in the wind, sagging, but not letting go.

Franklin felt as though all his muscles relaxed suddenly. His shoulder, where the thorn bush had impaled him, stopped hurting him. Hell, all the places where the thorns had bit him felt better.

What the hell was that doctor doing?

Even the wound from the knife felt better.

Was this what the doctor was raising souls for? Killing ghosts so he could heal the living?

It was a cheat, Franklin knew. But he could understand why the doctor was doing it, at least.

The doctor started chanting in that strange tongue of his, the words whipping the ghosts into shape, drawing them all in again. The howling of the ghosts thinned to a single wire of pain as they faded.

The knife grew more bloated, overly full and unhappy about it. It struggled to release the souls it had taken again, but the doctor held it firmly in his will.

Finally, the ghosts faded to nothing, the mist and the light dying.

The doctor sagged, but he still called out across the now empty hill, "Healed!"

He looked younger. The white fringes of his hair had red shot through it, now. Franklin hadn't noticed the age spots dotting the doctor's skull, not until they was all gone.

Was the doctor just trying to make himself young?

That didn't seem right. He wouldn't need a whole army of ghosts to do that.

Faster than Franklin would have thought, the doctor packed up. Franklin struggled with the trees again. They held fast, strong. Franklin turned to see Julie, who shook her head at him.

She didn't want them to go confront the doctor? But why?

Did she really know him? Was he that dangerous?

Franklin waited until the doctor had disappeared down the far side of the hill before he pulled at the tree limbs holding him again.

The trees reluctantly loosened. Franklin pulled his arms away, his skin sticky with pine sap.

He ran over to Julie, helping her pull her second arm away, then he wrapped himself around her, holding her close to his chest.

She smelled good, womanly and woodsy. Franklin knew it weren't appropriate, how much he wanted her, right then and there.

Julie seemed to realize, though, what he was feeling. Maybe she was feeling the same. She pulled him in for a long, deep kiss, before pushing him away.

"We need to get back into town," she whispered against his lips.

Franklin immediately loosened his grip around her. "Okay," he said. Disappointment filled him, but he understood.

The doctor had done something, something that weren't natural. And something he hadn't meant to do, with that burp of power. It was still affecting Franklin, in ways he didn't know or trust.

"Do you know who he is?" Franklin asked as Julie took his hand and they started hurrying out of the battlefield, back toward the car.

"Maybe," Julie said, nodding. "I want to look something up, first."

"Okay," Franklin said. He trusted her. They'd figure this out.

Then maybe take some time with each other.

FRANKLIN STOOD STILL, holding his shirt up around his chest while Julie examined him under the bright lights of his kitchen. It was late, and the ghosts that had been haunting Franklin had gone. Or at least, he didn't hear them howling outside anymore.

He didn't want to think about what the doctor had done to them, how he'd taken first their will, then possibly, their souls.

But at least the farm was quiet, just the cicadas and the crickets outside, the AC pumping cool air in the living room.

Franklin stretched, his muscles still loose. He should be tired, given the hour and what they'd been up to all day, but he wasn't. Not at all.

In fact, he still wanted Julie. So much. It was getting uncomfortable.

"That's what I thought," Julie said after a moment. She turned his face to the side. "You'd started getting a few gray hairs along your temples, just here," she added, lightly brushing her finger along his tightly kinky hair.

Franklin shivered at her gentle touch, closing his eyes.

"But it's all gone now. And you said you're mostly healed?" she asked.

"Yes, ma'am," Franklin said. He was afraid to take off his shirt all the way off though, afraid that might just make it harder not to touch her.

"That's what I thought," Julie said, carelessly running her finger down from his temple to his neck.

"What?" Franklin asked. He couldn't help himself. He caught her hand and kissed the back of it.

Now it was time for Julie to shiver.

"Come on," Julie said, taking Franklin's hand and squeezing it, leading him through the rest of the house, toward the bedroom.

"What?" Franklin asked. "I thought you wanted to look something up." He'd assumed she meant on the internet. Which meant going someplace else, since he didn't have no internet out at the farm. Hell, he barely got cell phone reception.

"That can wait until the morning," Julie said with a lovely, inviting smile. "Right now, I think you need a more thorough examine."

"Yes, ma'am," Franklin said, returning her smile and not worrying again about the doctor or ghosts or anything else until the sun had long risen.

KARL HAD ALREADY GIVEN Franklin the day off since he'd been stabbed, so Franklin wasn't concerned about getting to the fruit and vegetable stand early the next morning.

He just wouldn't tell Karl that he'd been miraculously healed, that the stitches had all dissolved, that all his bruises and aches and sores were already gone.

After breakfast, Julie insisted on stopping by the public library. She still needed to do some research on the internet.

The library was a newer building, built like Franklin's 1950s rambler, all one story, made of brick. The inside was all white, freshly painted, with the AC cranked high. Skylights lit the front desk area, with white metal stacks to one side holding newspapers and trade magazines, while at the end of the room sat three computers.

Franklin sat in one of the uncomfortable chairs next to the desk (it was too soft) and read about crop rotation while Julie pecked at the computer.

She looked lovely in a white T-shirt that showed off her curves and jeans that hung down low on her hips. Despite being up most of the night, she didn't look tired at all. Her soft brown hair had a nice curl in it, as though she'd spent hours futzing with it, though all she'd done was wash it and brush it out.

They both felt younger, healthy, well.

Was that the doctor's plan?

Finally, Julie called Franklin over to the terminal. A white teenager sat sullenly paging through some comic on one side, while the other side was open. Franklin borrowed that chair and pulled it up close to Julie.

The teenager glanced over, rolled his eyes, then determinedly looked at his screen again.

Julie mutely pointed to the page she'd pulled up.

The date on the article was three years old.

Franklin recognized the picture of the doctor right away, though it was a grainy photo, and the doctor had been ducking his head, as if trying to hide.

Underneath the picture listed his name.

Doctor Lamont Traeger. On his way to trial.

Where had Franklin heard that name before? He could swear it was familiar.

Franklin read through the article.

The doctor had been raised in Wesley county. Local boy done good. Gone off to medical school, promising surgeon.

Then tragedy had struck. First his wife had died, killed by a fast cancer that they'd discovered too late. Then his son had been killed in a pileup on the interstate, flattened between two semi's.

Franklin shook his head. Pure shame. He suspected that the doctor was the kind who wouldn't have had cousins and brothers and sisters to help him pull through. When he'd lost his wife and son, he'd really lost his whole family.

Dr. Traeger had kept working, though. Trying to heal others, despite how broken he was himself.

The newspaper story Julie had pulled up was all about a trial. The hospital where Dr. Traeger had been working accused him of "helping" a patient along. Labeled him an "Angel of Mercy."

Dr. Traeger maintained his innocence.

"So what happened?" Franklin asked Julie when he got to the end of the article. It had been written during the trial, not after the case had been settled.

The teenager glared at them and Franklin lowered his voice. "Was he found guilty?"

Julie shook her head, frowning. "I can't find anything about it. It's like the articles got all taken down. But I don't think he was found guilty. If I'm remembering right, he was just forced to retire. Claimed it was politics that got to him. But there was talk at the nurse's station, one night. They all thought he was guilty as sin. Not just helping patients who needed help, but ones that weren't ready yet."

Franklin nodded, not surprised. Most doctors seemed to think they knew better than everyone.

"I know that name from someplace," Franklin said as he followed Julie out of the library. "Dr. Lamont Traeger."

"From the trial?" Julie asked.

Franklin shook his head. "No. Recent like. I just can't remember when."

"It'll come to you," Julie told him, taking his hand.

Franklin opened his mouth to say something to her, something about her, about them, but then closed it again. It wasn't the right time or place.

He knew he was stalling.

But maybe later that night...

"So what's the plan?" Franklin asked as he got into Julie's car.

"I'm gonna drop you back off at the farm, then go in to work," Julie said. "I'll try and talk with some of the older nurses, see if I can find out anything."

"You coming by later tonight?" Franklin asked, trying to hide his disappointment. He'd hoped they'd be able to spend the day together.

"I should probably get some sleep tonight," Julie said.

"Oh," Franklin said. He thought a moment, then still decided to ask his question. "Are you feeling tired?"

"Not really," Julie admitted. "But after work there are still a few things I want to check."

"All right," Franklin said. They rode in silence back to the farm, comfortable with each other. "What's your schedule like the rest of the week?"

"Working mainly afternoons," Julie told him. "So maybe I can come over tomorrow night."

"It's a date," Franklin told her, drawing her over for a sweet goodbye kiss that quickly got out of hand.

When they finally pulled back, Franklin was aching for Julie like he'd never felt before.

"Do you think that's part of what Dr. Traeger did? To make us so horny?" Julie asked.

"No," Franklin said immediately. "Okay, maybe a little," he said after another moment. "But I've always wanted you like this. I just hid it."

Silence filled the car. Had he said too much?

But then Julie gave him another of those toe-curling kisses. "Me too," she whispered against his lips.

Then she pulled back. "Now, shoo. I'll see you tomorrow night."

Franklin opened the car door, then turned back. "You know there's only you, right? In my world?" he asked earnestly.

"I know, darling," she replied, caressing his cheek. "And we can talk about that more tomorrow night."

Franklin knew he was pushing it, but he still gave her one last light kiss on her nose before getting out of the car.

It was gonna feel like tomorrow night would never come, he knew.

It were also gonna come way too fast, for what he had in mind.

~

FRANKLIN SPENT the day working around the farm, taking away the stalks that the ghosts had trampled (and had it been the ghosts? Or had Dr. Traeger come and done it?) and putting them on the compost pile, applying WD-40 to that door hinge that kept squeaking, encouraging the yellow jackets who liked the southern eves of the house to go nest somewhere else.

He also did laundry and put fresh sheets on the bed. Just in case Julie changed her mind and came by that night anyway.

But he spent the night alone and slept much better than he had in a week or so, waking up refreshed and ready to tackle the world.

He came out to the kitchen to make sure everything was in order for dinner that night—he was making Mama's spaghetti with his secret ingredient: grape jelly. He had candles out on the table in Mama's fancy silver holders, wine glasses with a tasty box of white wine already chilling in the fridge, and he was gonna get out the good china.

He wasn't about to propose to Julie—that was way too soon. But he did plan on telling her just how much he loved her.

No regular ghosts waited for him outside, but he still checked his bicycle before he got on it. The trip to the fruit and vegetable stand were easy that morning, as if Franklin had been doing his regular exercises.

Was he younger, now, after the doctor's spell? How long would it last?

Karl gave Franklin a long look and just shook his head when he came pedaling up. For the first time, Franklin noticed that Karl had some white in his goatee, not just brown.

Karl was a young man, like Franklin, in his late twenties. How long would he feel young? How long before he started looking and acting old?

When they'd finished serving the morning rush, Karl came over to Franklin. "So you got stabbed," he said dourly.

"Yeah," Franklin said. "Damn doctor—Dr. Traeger—wanted a knife that I had."

Franklin weren't sure how much he should tell Karl about what he'd been up to.

"Well, you look better than you did all week last week," Karl said.

Franklin nodded. "The loud, howling ghosts is finally gone." If Franklin were some kind of Catholic or religious like what he'd seen on TV, he might have made the sign of the cross or something. *God rest their souls.*

Though he didn't know if those poor dead people had any souls left, or if the doctor had eaten them all up.

"There something else I should know about?" Karl asked after another moment.

"I'm not sure," Franklin said honestly. His business with the doctor wasn't finished yet, but he had no idea what they was gonna do next.

"Okay," Karl said. "But you need more time off, you let me know."

"Same for you," Franklin said, since they was partners in this venture.

Karl gave him a big grin. "I might at that. There's this new checker at the pharmacy…"

"You gonna actually ask her out?" Franklin asked. That had been Karl's problem for a while now, admiring girls but not following through.

"I aim to," Karl said. "Might need to leave early Friday."

"Plan on it, then," Franklin said. "I'll hold down the fort here."

"Thanks," Karl said. "How you and Miss Julie doing?"

Franklin felt his cheeks flush. "We're doing just fine." He was gonna tell her he loved her and everything.

"That's good to hear," Karl said. "All right. I'm outta here. I'll be back later this afternoon."

Karl turned to go, then paused, and turned back. "Wait a minute. Did you say Dr. Traeger? Lamont Traeger?"

"Yeah," Franklin said slowly. How did Karl know the doctor's first name? Franklin hadn't mentioned it, he was sure.

When Karl beckoned, Franklin walked to his side, then stared at the police charity ball poster Karl was pointing at.

Franklin was about to ask what Karl was going on about when he saw it.

There, at the bottom of the poster, in the fine print.

Dr. Traeger was listed as one of the sponsors of the ball.

Then Franklin read further.

Hell, the ball was gonna be out at Dr. Traeger's estate. That Saturday night. Three nights from then.

No wonder that name had sounded so familiar.

Was that why the doctor had all those ghosts trapped in that blade? So he could make all those rich people young and healthy again?

Franklin was just gonna have to stop him. It weren't right, him killing all those ghosts, stealing their peace.

But how?

CHAPTER 8

JULIE ARRIVED RIGHT AT SEVEN. Pretty orange and pink clouds spread all the way across the horizon, and the edges were a deep red. Franklin had never considered leaving Kentucky, and sunsets like this one were part of the reason why.

He had everything prepared for Julie—the pasta, the sauce, the garlic bread—he'd even put flowers, wild red roses and white peonies on the kitchen table.

Julie took one look at it all and turned and walked right back out of the kitchen, out the front door.

Franklin hurried out after her.

She was wearing a tight purple T-shirt made of a silky material that Franklin liked to touch, with her good jeans, the ones that showed off her curves. So Franklin knew she'd been looking forward to the date.

"What's wrong?" Franklin asked, coming up quietly behind Julie.

She stood on the edge of the front porch, looking out over the driveway and her old beater Ford.

"Just that," Julie said. She waved one arm back toward the house, then wrapped them both tightly across her chest.

Were those tears in her eyes?

"I didn't mean to upset you," Franklin said. He slowly slid his own arms around her from the back, watching carefully for any sign that he should stop.

"I just wanted to make you a nice dinner," he added when she'd been quiet for a long moment.

"Now, Franklin Kanly, don't be lying to me," Julie scolded. "You had something else planned."

Franklin wanted to make a joke about spending another long night together, but even he knew now wasn't the time. "I'd been wanted to tell you how much you mean to me," he admitted.

It somehow seemed easier, telling her like this, without having to look at her face, so Franklin continued.

"How much I love you, and want to be with you," Franklin continued, his voice a hoarse whisper.

Just 'cause it were easier, didn't make it easy.

Julie turned in Franklin's arms and wrapped herself around him. She held on fiercely tight, and Franklin did the same.

She was crying.

He didn't know what to do, except pet her hair and kiss her temple now and again, waiting out the storm.

"I went to see the doctor today. My gynecologist," Julie said.

"That's a woman's doctor, right?" Franklin asked, wanting to make sure he understood.

He felt her nod against his wet shirt.

"Regular checkup. Except that it weren't regular. They did an ultrasound. Said there's something wrong with my cervix. Something blocking it." Julie took a deep breath then let it out in a loud sigh. "Said if they can't fix it, I might not ever be able to have kids."

"You know I'll love you anyway, right?" Franklin said.

Though he thought he'd said the right thing, Julie started crying again.

Franklin couldn't help but get more tense. Had he said it wrong? Was he not supposed to say it?

"Oh you idiot," Julie said, wrapping her arms more tightly around Franklin and holding on as he started to pull away. "I suspected you might say something like that. Or I hoped you would."

"Course I would," Franklin said. He weren't the kind of man to leave a woman if she couldn't have children. He didn't know what they'd do. Would they adopt? Get some special surgery? He knew a woman in the next county who had other people's kids for them. She used to come in to have Mama do her nails regularly.

But the pair of them would cross that bridge when they got there.

Julie sniffed and wiped at her nose with the back of her hand. "You know I love you too, right?" she asked quietly.

"I was hoping you'd say something like that," Franklin said.

That finally got him a smile.

"The doctor said he hadn't seen anything like it before," Julie said. "It's why they want to give me more tests. It's like the opening to my uterus got blocked off by extra skin."

Franklin grew very still. "Julie, do you think it might have happened the night before? That blast from Doctor Traeger that healed us? Made us feel younger?"

Julie paused, then nodded. "I hadn't thought of that. But you may be right. My period was supposed to start any day now. Now, it looks like I won't be having any for a while."

Franklin nodded, trying to put it all together. "So this doctor, he ain't cheating death. He wants to beat it. Make everyone young and healthy all the time. He said something about no more death. And no more birth." Franklin paused, then added, "That battlefield was just a test of how many souls he could raise at once. He's throwing a charity ball, you know?"

Julie shook her head.

"That's where I'd heard his name before. He's gonna have a bunch of people at his place, people who have paid him a lot of money."

"Then what'll he do?" Julie asked. "Make them all young again?"

"More than that," Franklin said. "He's a doctor. He don't want to just cheat death. He wants to beat it." He was planning to subvert the natural process.

It just weren't right.

"He's stealing the lives of ghosts to do it," Julie added.

"Which most folks wouldn't mind," Franklin pointed out. He'd mind, but most folks didn't know better.

Julie looked back at him, surprised. "Really?"

Franklin shrugged. "They're dead, right? They've had their chance. Why worry about the dead now?" It wasn't how he felt, but he could already hear the commentators on the TV talking about it, how they'd justify what they was doing.

"People don't know he's stealing their souls with that blade," Julie pointed out.

"Exactly," Franklin said. "We got to get that blade away from him. Folks don't always do the right thing, particularly when they don't have all the facts."

"I'll help," Julie said.

Franklin paused, then said, "Okay."

Though he knew he was lying to her.

It wasn't that he was gonna steal that blade back all by himself. No, he'd have help. But he weren't about to do something that illegal with her. Or something that might be dangerous.

But Darryl would help. Hell, he might even be useful for once.

Julie lay quietly in Franklin's arms, but he knew she wasn't sleeping. They'd had a real nice dinner, and a real nice afterwards, too.

"You think it would be that bad? Living forever?" Julie finally asked.

"That isn't the problem," Franklin said. "I wouldn't mind living forever with you," he added, kissing her temple. "But it seems like part of the price is that there won't be anyone new. No births. Remember? Just those people who get made immortal. And, well, that would be it. That would be all the people there ever was."

Julie nodded against his chest. "I think that would grow old," she said.

He could hear the smile in her voice. He kissed her hair again.

Then he sighed, thinking about the consequences.

"No new kids. No new babies to smile at. No one to teach nothing to," Franklin said, his voice growing hoarse with emotion. No new families.

"No Mother's Day flowers. No princess tea parties in the backyard," Julie continued.

No son to teach the proper methods of popping corn to. No daughter to be proud of and brag on.

Franklin would never know what it was like to be a dad. Since he'd never had one, not really, as his dad had died just after Franklin had been born, he'd always planned on being a really good dad, there all the time.

If the doctor won, Franklin would never have the chance.

"We'll stop him," Julie said curling up against Franklin's side, her breath deepening into sleep.

Franklin stayed awake for a while longer, holding onto this precious time. He understood the temptation to stay just in one place. But wasn't that what his duty was? To help ghosts—people —move along?

Doctor Traeger was planning on using that blade, that soul taker, to beat death.

Franklin was determined to not let the doctor win.

DARRYL SHOWED up at Franklin's house right after work, wearing his car mechanic's uniform. Franklin wasn't sure how much Darryl was getting done at the job with his arm still in a sling.

He expected Darryl wasn't resting his arm like he should be. But Franklin weren't his cousin May, and wasn't about to harangue him about it. Plus, Darryl's wife Georgia was likely to be giving Darryl an earful already.

Darryl didn't look like he'd been working, though. Normally, he were covered in grease and Franklin always had to insist that he wash his hands. Twice.

"Got me up front, minding the register," Darryl said after he'd changed into a gray, short-sleeved, button-up shirt and jeans. (Seemed a T-shirt was just too much trouble with his arm.)

"Bet that just makes your day," Franklin said dryly.

Darryl shrugged. "It ain't been too bad, actually," he said.

Franklin wondered if Darryl's own dark skin were hiding his blush.

"I don't have much of a head for numbers, but I have been working inventory, making sure we actually have what we need for parts," Darryl added, boasting.

"What, they discover the hick has a brain?" Franklin teased.

Darryl just rolled his eyes. "I may not be as smart as Jason—none of us is. But I know what I know."

"That you do," Franklin said.

"So what exactly are we hunting?" Darryl asked.

"Two things, actually," Franklin said. "First, can you come look at something?"

Franklin hadn't felt as though anyone had been watching him the week before he went to get the blade from Darryl. But how else had Dr. Traeger known about ghosts Franklin had helped?

They tromped outside. The sun had just set and the night seemed lighter, while the sound of trucks on the interstate a mile away seemed heavier, a stream of them, probably all racing for their dinner. Fresh dirt smells and green grass filled the air. The chorus of frogs was just starting up.

Just a little ways up from the driveway, along the ditch on Franklin's property, Franklin thought he'd spotted something.

"That look like a hunting nest to you?" he asked Darryl.

Darryl squatted down and waved his hand over the bent grass. Then he broke off one of the stems, brought it up to his nose and got a good sniff.

"Seems someone's been watching you," Darryl said. His voice took on a deeper timbre.

Franklin nodded. That was what he'd been afraid of. He hadn't noticed the bent grass until the other day, when he'd spent time fixing stuff all around the farm.

Darryl stood up, then turned first one way, then the other. Without warning he took off, running with that grace that meant he was doing the one thing he'd been born to do: hunt things.

Darryl raced back along the ditch to Franklin's driveway, then up, toward the lane.

Franklin took off after his cousin. Even though he were still feeling younger, he knew he'd never keep up. Not when Darryl was running with his full powers.

Darryl had turned up the lane, toward the empty Averson fields. He stopped after about a quarter mile.

"Think he parked here," Darryl said, growling. He paced the area, frustrated. "Can't really chase a scent in a car," he said. He turned back to Franklin and shook his head. "You got an idea who was doing this? Invading your privacy like this?"

"Yeah, I do," Franklin said sourly. "Figure it was the same guy who stabbed me."

"Stabbed you?" Darryl asked. He was suddenly right there beside Franklin, running his hands up and down about an inch away from Franklin's body.

His hand stopped right at Franklin's side, where he'd been injured. Where had Darryl learned to do that?

"With that blade. The one that had been buried under your thorn bush." Franklin explained, turning back down the lane and heading toward his farmhouse. "He was waiting for me that night, after we dug it out."

Darryl gave a low, long whistle, stepping back. "So you never used it?"

Franklin shook his head. "Nope."

"Good," Darryl said. "That blade weren't good."

"But it weren't bad, either," Franklin said. "It depends on the *intent* of the person who's holding it."

What do you mean?" Darryl asked.

"I learned some of the history of the knife. It been made to take souls, use them in sacrifice," Franklin said.

"That don't sound good to me," Darryl said, looking wary.

"If I used it to encourage souls to pass on, that would be cheating, but it wouldn't be bad," Franklin pointed out.

"I don't know, Cuz," Darryl said. "I still think it's evil."

"Well, it might be a bit more powerful, right now," Franklin admitted.

"You're joking," Darryl said.

Franklin explained about how the doctor was using it to steal the souls of the dead, raising up an army of ghosts, and how the blade now was overfull with all of them.

"He's gonna use it to make all the rich and powerful people live forever?" Darryl asked, agitated. He looked like he really wanted to shoot something.

"That's what I think," Franklin said. "So we got to go steal that blade back."

"Do you know where this knife is?" Darryl asked.

"I do," Franklin said. Despite being healed, he still had a connection to the knife, could still feel its cold blade in his side.

"What do you need me for then?" Darryl said. "If you don't need me to go hunting for it?"

"I figure there will be traps out there," Franklin said. "And that you might know how to break into someplace bettern me."

Finally, Darryl gave Franklin a big smile. "That I do. Let's go steal us a blade."

DR. TRAEGER LIVED west of Katherinesville, along an old country lane that was barely two-cars wide. If someone came the other way, they'd both end up with their far tires on the shoulder to pass.

The land along the lane was all fields, open and green. It was too dark to see the quality of the crops, but they seemed to be doing well. The moon was only half-full, and even in clear areas didn't provide much light.

Red brick columns stood on either side of the drive leading to the Traeger estate. Beyond them grew tall, graceful oaks, forming an arch.

Franklin would bet that this used to be a plantation. Was probably old money.

Had the doctor started here? Using the ghosts of the dead from his own land?

Franklin shivered. They had to get that blade away from him, make it more difficult for him to steal souls.

Darryl drove by the entrance slowly, casing the joint, as it were.

"Place is too big to have a fence all the way around it," he said after they'd gone a ways and hadn't come to another driveway.

How many acres did the doctor own?

"All the security will be up closer to the house," Darryl added as he turned around. He found a wide flat shoulder to pull his truck onto about a quarter mile from the front entrance.

"Any idea what kind he might have? What we should be looking for?" Franklin asked as he slid out of the truck.

Darryl shrugged one-armed, not moving the shoulder with the sling. "Beats me. You said he's raising ghosts?"

Franklin nodded grimly as Darryl dug into the back of his truck, hauling out a backpack and thrusting it at Franklin.

"That might be the only protection he needs, if they start howling at the approach of strangers," Darryl pointed out.

"Don't think it works that way," Franklin said. "They howl all the damn time."

Darryl paused by the side of the road, sniffing the air. "Don't think he keeps dogs," he said. "I'll smell 'em 'bout the time they smell us."

Franklin nodded, impressed. He hadn't been sure if Darryl would have embraced his gift or if he would have gone on denying it.

Seemed his cousin had really been working with it. They was gonna have to sit down with some beers sometime, and Darryl was gonna have to tell some tales. Or maybe go hunting, after Darryl was fully healed, just to see.

The cousins crossed the lane then started up onto the property. Huge trees with massive brambles and bushes worked as good as a fence next to the road. However, Darryl could find the single path through them easily enough, without hesitation.

After the thick bush, the land opened up. Just trees grew there, huge old oaks, with roots raised up almost a foot off the ground, looking to trip anyone walking. Of course, Darryl didn't have any problem, but Franklin stumbled more than once.

Was the trees trying to stop them? Slow them down? Franklin remembered the pines at Perryville.

But these oaks weren't moving on their own. They was slow and sleepy. It was just Franklin's own two feet and the dark of the night that were the problem.

Darryl led them unerringly toward the house. Franklin might have been able to do that too, given the way he still felt connected to that blade. It was sleeping, kind of, or at least resting. It still felt bloated, overly full, and tired.

It was still carrying far too many souls around. The blade wanted rid of them. It felt ill-used.

It didn't like the doctor one bit.

Maybe Franklin could use that, get the blade to turn against the doctor. Not like the blade could move on its own, though.

Up closer to the house came the first wall—a tall one, made of old brick. It bulged toward the bottom, the weight of its age forcing the bricks out of their straight lines. It had been patched in place, though, and was still strong. Franklin didn't see any barbed wire running along the top of it—or any cameras.

"Can we go around?" Franklin asked, crouching down next to Darryl at the foot of the wall. It was at least seven feet tall.

"We're gonna have to," Darryl said grimly. "I just can't make it over."

While Franklin was strong, and maybe he could get over that wall on his own, he couldn't pull Darryl up after him.

Darryl placed his free hand on the wall, sliding it to the right, bumping over the old brick, then to the left.

Franklin could see something tugging on Darryl's hand, until the fingers all pointed toward the left.

"This way," Darryl said, easily hopping over a bush growing up next to the wall.

Just a ways down, an old wooden door led through the wall. The doorway was arched, with a fancy brick pattern of interlocking diamonds done in stone above it. The door itself had three, rusting iron bars running across it, holding it together.

The door handle was brand new, the shiny silver looking out of place. A metal plate surrounded the handle and ran to the edge of the door. Franklin figured that was to make it extra strong. He'd bet that the hole the lock slid into was all metal as well.

Darryl fished his keys out of his pockets, then held up a strange-looking key, longer than a regular one, with just small nibs on either side. "Proper skeleton key," he said. It didn't take him but three tries and they were through the door.

"Are those legal?" Franklin asked as Darryl paused and wiped their fingerprints from the shiny metal.

Darryl shrugged. "They ain't illegal," he said. "Now, a bump key? That'll get you some hard questioning."

Franklin weren't sure what that was. He also weren't sure Darryl didn't happen to have one of those on him, either. He weren't about to ask, though.

The yard on the other side of the brick wall seemed quieter, and the night seemed thicker. Even the cicadas weren't as loud.

They was standing on soft dirt, between two big azaleas still dotted with pink flowers. A garden grew next to the wall, a three foot wide strip, covered in cedar mulch and filled with tamed shrubs. Beyond that was the yard proper, with neatly trimmed grass, more stately oaks, and a screened-in gazebo to the left.

The air held the smell of the cedar and the grass and good, rich soil.

To the right stood a tall old house, made of wood with a steep jutting roof—Franklin guessed, the plantation. It'd probably be right pretty in the daylight; right now, it was just a dark shape. Beside it was a more modern, square building, just a single story made of brick, but huge. Twice as long as the house. Big enough to hold one of those Olympic swimming pools.

That was probably where they'd be having the charity ball.

The blade was in the house, maybe on one of the upper floors.

Franklin was about to step out of the patch of garden and onto the lawn when Darryl held him back.

"Not that way," Darryl whispered. Instead, he crept along the mulch, close to the wall.

Of course, there would be roses there, old ones, with canes thicker than Franklin's thumb—more thorns digging into Franklin's skin. Darryl passed without a scratch.

When Darryl paused for a moment, Franklin asked him, "Why we going this way?"

Darryl pointed straight up.

On top of the wall was a black glass dome that Franklin hadn't seen from the other side.

Franklin recognized it as one of those fancy security cameras. Charlene had installed them all over the grocery store where he'd used to work. He shivered.

He weren't sure that hiding next to the wall would keep them out of sight. But stepping onto the lawn they'd absolutely be seen.

Darryl led them as close to the house as they could get along the garden part of the wall. Then he backed them up about three feet.

"The cameras don't have as good an angle, here," Darryl explained.

Franklin weren't sure where Darryl had learned about that sort of thing. It wasn't part of his hunting gift.

"Follow me. Step where I do," Darryl instructed.

Franklin felt completely exposed once they left the bushes of the garden, like a deer in an open meadow with hunters nearby. But he followed Darryl, walking sideways along the yard, keeping his back to the camera on his right.

They'd almost made it all the way across the yard to the porch when a bright light came on.

"Hold it right there."

CHAPTER 9

FRANKLIN DIDN'T SAY nothing to Darryl as they rode in the back of the police car into town.

What could he say? They'd failed, big time. Been caught trespassing.

The doctor was much more prepared than they were.

Franklin didn't know how he was gonna get that blade from Dr. Traeger before Saturday night. But he'd have to find a way.

They hadn't seen Dr. Traeger that night. It had been his security guard who'd stopped them, a white man with a doughy face who looked like he never smiled. He'd held a gun on them, just itching for an excuse to shoot.

Franklin had been processed once at the judicial center in town, when Karl had threatened to charge him for trespassing. It was just as bad the second time. He hated getting his fingerprints taken—that aggravated him more than any other part of the process. The smell of the ink got under his skin, though Darryl said there weren't no smell to it.

Then they sat in the holding cell for the rest of the night. It was made of long cold bars on two side, attached to the corner of the general judicial center. Ordinary desks filled the rest of the room, most of them filled with stacks of papers and humming computer monitors.

Being there overnight was more wearing on Darryl than on Franklin. He was still healing. So Franklin stayed awake, letting Darryl stretch out on the single cot across the back wall.

His cousin didn't look any younger when he was sleeping—he didn't have that many lines in his face that needed smoothing out. He had the same brow as Franklin, broad and wide. Made him look intelligent, smarter than your average hick. His nose was more broad, flatter, and his lips was fatter too.

Franklin could see how Darryl's boys shared their father's look.

If the doctor won and cheated death like he planned, Franklin would never be able to see his face in his boy's. Would never know if his daughter's eyes would look like his. Would never see Mama's smile there either.

Around eight o'clock the next morning, long after the rest of the officers had arrived, Sheriff Thompson came in. He stood on the far side of the bars and glared at the pair of them.

"I thought I told you to keep your nose clean," he growled at Franklin.

"Yes, sir," Franklin said.

"What was you doing down at Dr. Traeger's?" the sheriff asked.

Franklin opened his mouth, only to find his arm grabbed and pinched. Hard.

"Ow!" he said, staring at a now wide-awake Darryl.

"Nothing," Darryl said. "We weren't doing anything."

Franklin was impressed by just how much scorn the sheriff managed to convey by just rolling his eyes. "Really? Nothing?"

Franklin wisely kept his mouth shut. He'd let Darryl handle this.

His cousin had a lot more experience on this side of the bars than Franklin did.

"What, you was just out joy riding? Got lost?" Sheriff Thompson asked.

That was what Darryl had dictated to Franklin to put in his report. His own was identical. Probably word for word.

"That's it exactly," Darryl said. After a moment, he added, "Sir."

"You know the security tape shows you sneaking in and creeping along the fence. And those are some awfully interesting keys you got on your key ring," Sheriff Thompson said.

"I work in a garage. You know how people are always locking their keys in their car," Darryl said brazenly.

"That's what a slim-jim's for," the sheriff pointed out.

Darryl just shrugged.

"And you, Franklin? You got anything to say for yourself?" Sheriff Thompson asked, fixing his hard stare on him.

"No, sir," Franklin said. "We was just out. Driving."

"You know what I think?" Sheriff Thompson asked. When neither man replied, he continued. "I think you saw all those posters about the charity ball. And the silent auction. And just decided you might help yourself to a few of those items, before they was auctioned off."

"Really?" Franklin asked. He couldn't help himself. He was boggled. Did the sheriff really think that low of him? "You really think I'd go stealing other people's property?"

Though that had been exactly what he'd been going to do. Kinda. Though actually, he'd just been going to take back what had been stolen from him.

Sheriff Thompson didn't budge. "You tell me."

Franklin sat back, crossing his arms over his chest, disgusted. He'd thought the sheriff knew better.

"Well, you two are just lucky. Dr. Traeger decided not to press any charges," the sheriff said after a few moments of silence. "Y'all are free to go."

Franklin stood up stiffly, not meeting the sheriff's eye. Darryl looked happy, giving the sheriff a wide grin as he stepped from the cell.

The sheriff stopped Franklin from following. "What was you really after?" he asked.

"You wouldn't believe me if I told you," Franklin said.

"Probably not," the sheriff said. "Try me."

"That Dr. Traeger is the same one who stabbed me," Franklin said. "He has my knife."

The sheriff nodded, smoothing down his mustache thoughtfully with his forefinger and thumb. "I figured that's what you'd say," he said. "And you're right, I don't believe you."

Franklin shook his head and stood there, staring holes at the floor.

"But if you can bring me some proof," the sheriff said softly, "I'd think better of you."

Franklin couldn't help but roll his own eyes at that one. No matter what he did, Sheriff Thompson was always gonna give him a hard time.

"I know you don't believe me," the sheriff said as he stepped out of the way so Franklin could leave. "But I'm not the bad guy here. I'm not out to get you."

Franklin knew that. The sheriff was just doing his job.

Unfortunately, that meant he was protecting the bad guy.

Franklin would just have to find another way to get the blade away from the doctor.

Before it was too late.

~

KARL GAVE Franklin a mean look as he came pedaling up that morning, as if they weren't partners and competitors anymore, but some kind of enemies.

Franklin had no intention of telling Karl where he'd been all night. On the one hand, Franklin didn't want to lie to Karl about having ghosts who needed his help.

On the other hand, what other excuse did Franklin have for arriving so late to the fruit and vegetable stand?

There were a lot of people at the stand for a Thursday morning. So Franklin got right to work, helping customers, picking out the ripest tomatoes for Mrs. Beckons who came by at least twice a week, as well as chatting with some tourists who couldn't get over how green everything was.

By the time the crowd had died down, Karl no longer looked like he was hopping mad. Still, his arms and back under his tight white T-shirt were all tense and knotted.

"I'm sorry I was so late, Karl," Franklin started off with. He figured that were always the best way to begin this kind of thing, though he had no intention of telling Karl all of his troubles.

They were competitors, still getting to know each other. They weren't best friends, for all that they did hang out together now.

Karl sighed and crossed his arms over his chest. He looked mad. And kinda twitchy, like he was just looking for something to hit.

"Sheriff Thompson stopped by early this morning, told me you might be late," Karl said sourly. "You want to tell me what the hell is going on?"

Franklin opened his mouth, then closed it. Them kinda cuss words shouldn't be said out loud.

"I got caught trespassing," Franklin said after a moment. "But they didn't press any charges."

Karl nodded. "Why," he asked flatly.

"You remember I was stabbed by a blade that was stolen?" Franklin asked.

"You sure don't look like you've been stabbed," Karl said.

"That's a whole other story," Franklin said. "But I found out who took that knife. And what they're gonna do with it. So Darryl and I went to go steal it back."

Karl bit his lips together for a moment. It looked like he was gonna explode.

"Darryl. And you. Trying to break into someplace that has some kind of security?" Karl couldn't seem to hold it in any longer. He started laughing. "I woulda bought tickets to watch that."

"Well, we failed," Franklin said. He and Darryl weren't that much of a screwup.

"I'm sorry," Karl said after he stopped laughing. "That's just too much."

"We still need to get that blade back," Franklin said seriously. "It's important."

"How important?" Karl asked.

"Matter of life and death for a lot of folks," Franklin replied. He weren't about to explain that it meant the death of a bunch of ghosts —that would just complicate matters.

"Maybe you should hire an expert," Karl said slowly.

"You know one?" Franklin asked. Karl knew a lot more people than Franklin expected him to. He was always greeting people at the stand, people Franklin would have never expected to see there.

"You remember Harvey Alturez?" Karl asked. "From high school?"

Franklin nodded. Somewhere along the line Harvey's family had some Spanish blood. It showed up in Harvey's black hair and olive skin. He'd also been one of the tallest kids in school. Hated basketball, though.

"He's got a history with the law, breaking and entering, things like that," Karl said. He paused, considering. "But I don't think he's available. Seem to recall Mrs. Alturez saying he was back in jail."

"You know anyone else?" Franklin asked, thinking about the other people they knew from high school. Franklin had always kept his nose clean, never gotten on the wrong side of the law. Mama would have tanned his hide if he had.

Plus, Franklin had been working with a lot of ghosts, which had made high school even harder.

"No," Karl said after a moment. "But Ray might."

"Ray Donovan?" Franklin asked. He'd been the class brain, valedictorian, but generally well liked. Franklin thought Ray had left Kentucky years ago to make his fortune out in California.

"No," Karl said, exasperated. "Ray Sorrel. He used to be a fixer out in Hollywood. You needed something done, you went to Ray. He knows everybody. Both here and in Hollywood."

"I was planning on going to see him sometime," Franklin said slowly. "I try to invite him over to dinner on a regular basis."

"Ray will probably know someone. But it'll cost ya," Karl warned.

"That's okay," Franklin said. "Ray owes me."

And he did, for the times Franklin had gone over to help Adrianna.

However, Franklin hadn't been able to stop the creature. It had killed Adrianna. Ray didn't blame Franklin for that. That creature was the one to blame.

Still, Franklin hoped Ray wouldn't think it unseemly for him to ask for a favor.

He needed all the help he could get.

FRANKLIN TOOK his afternoon break and pedaled into Katherinesville, then turned up Stewart, going north, heading up toward the Sorrels' place. The outside of the gate used to be a continuation of Adrianna's "found" art: an old tin medicine cabinet with the door removed, filled with dolls' heads; rusty exhaust pipes welded together into long strange waves; even plastic bags tied together into faded streamers.

Ray had taken most of that down after she'd died. All that remained was the fancy doorbell next to the gate, made of blue-green brass swirls, with the button sitting in the heart of it like a lighted pearl.

Franklin pressed the button. The gate buzzed and unlocked, swinging open immediately.

Seemed as though Ray wanted company.

There was great speculation as to whether Ray would still have the picnic that he and Adrianna had hosted every year later that summer, inviting the whole town as usual, or if he'd not celebrate at all.

Franklin didn't know either, though he'd been one of the few people to step inside their property since Adrianna had died.

Ray had left a lot of Adrianna's artwork there, like the collection of outboard motors painted all the colors of the rainbow, up on fancy pillars; the odd-looking robot-man made out of spare car parts with holding an upturned hubcap filled with water for the birds; and the white rock paths that were laid along the lines of energy that Adrianna saw.

But a lot of it was gone, too, like the tree men who Adrianna had treated like her own grandchildren, who had tried to protect her from the creature, as well as the mural of the mermaid, made out of a mosaic of found glass shards, and the huge koi pond.

Franklin walked his bike inside the gate—leaving it outside was just asking for it to be stolen—and leaned it up against the fence.

Ray came out of the house. He'd always had gray hair, but he hadn't seemed old, necessarily. Adrianna's death had aged him, put lines in his square face, across his brow, over his bushy white eyebrows, along the sides of his mouth. He had a hard jaw that had just gotten harder, with teeth so white they couldn't be natural.

But he smiled when he saw Franklin, making him seem a bit younger. He still wore his favorite loud Hawaiian shirt, shorts, and brown socks with sandals, showing off his knobby knees.

"Franklin!" Ray said, holding out his hand.

Franklin shook it, glad to feel the strength of Ray.

"It's good to see you," Ray said after a moment. "You look well."

"Thank you," Franklin said. "So do you."

"I've been trying to keep busy. Well, busier. It's been helping," Ray said honestly. "Would you like some sweet tea?"

"Yes, please," Franklin said, following Ray into the house.

The living room seemed dark after the bright sunlight, so Franklin paused for a moment to let his eyes adjust. He was glad he did—the room had more furniture in it than he remembered. He would have walked right into a tall wing-back chair set just before the door if he'd just gone straight in. Plus, boxes sat stacked all around it.

Shelves lined the wall to Franklin's right, while a couch and love seat took up the walls on his left.

Adrianna hadn't spent as much time inside the house as out in the yard, so it held fewer of her touches. Still, the shelves in the living room proudly displayed the odd purple dragon she'd melded together out of found toys, the tall feather "plant," and the collection of soap logos she'd pasted together into a huge smiley face.

Beyond the living room was an open kitchen, with just an island separating it from the living room. To the left were large glass doors, leading to the backyard.

Ray fixed Franklin his tea, opened up a beer for himself, then led Franklin back out into the yard through the side door.

Once they got settled into the lawn chairs out there (the ones that Adrianna hated but let Ray keep), Franklin asked Ray, "How are you doing?"

"I'm doing okay," Ray said. "As I said, keeping myself busy helps."

The death of Adrianna still sat like an open wound on Ray's chest. Franklin weren't sure what he or anyone else could do.

"I'm glad you came by," Ray said. "I was going to talk with you about possibly storing some of Adrianna's things at your farm."

"Of course," Franklin said immediately. He didn't have any room, but he'd find some. Or make some. He'd been wanting to replace the old shed in the driveway with something fancier.

"Any reason in particular?" Franklin asked when Ray didn't continue. Was Ray planning on moving away? There had been those boxes in the living room…

Ray nodded slowly, taking another sip of his beer. "Katherinesville had never been my ideal retirement place. Adrianna needed to be here, though. She loved this place, so much." He took a deep breath.

Franklin waited patiently, giving Ray the space he needed to continue.

"But I think it's time for me to be moving on. I wasn't planning on selling this place," Ray hurried to say. "Although…I might just keep it as a vacation home. Live somewhere else. Maybe move someplace further south. Actually retire, like, to Florida."

Franklin knew that once Ray left, he'd never come back. The memories for him was just too painful.

"Just let me know what I can do to help," Franklin said sincerely.

"Thanks, Franklin," Ray said. "You've been a good friend these last months."

"I've tried," Franklin said. And he had. He'd invited Ray over for dinner at least once a month, and had stopped by his house more often than that.

He didn't know if Ray would ever stop mourning Adrianna.

"So how's Julie doing?" Ray asked with a smile that didn't seem as sad.

"She's doing well," Franklin said. "We're…we're doing well."

"That's good!" Ray said. "I hope we're going to be hearing some wedding bells soon."

Franklin opened his mouth then shut it again. Then he shrugged. "Possibly," was all he'd say.

Someday, he probably would marry Julie. There wasn't anyone else in his life who he'd ever loved that way, not even Mama.

Hell, he might even give up popcorn if she asked. Though she never would, which was partly why they got along so well.

"Just let me know the date. I'll be here," Ray said.

Franklin knew he meant it. "Thanks," Franklin said, taking a sip of his tea. He cleared his throat. Ray had asked him for a favor. Maybe that was the way to go…

"Speaking of favors…" Franklin said.

Ray nodded. "I didn't think this was just a social call. You seemed to have something on your mind. What is it?"

Ray had never seen Adrianna's lines of power, or Franklin's ghosts. Franklin had never really admitted to his powers to Ray. Ray had heard the stories, that Franklin always denied.

However, Ray knew something about the supernatural.

He had seen the creature.

"Someone stole something from me," Franklin said. "A powerful blade."

"Powerful how?" Ray asked.

"It can hold spirits, take them," Franklin said.

"I see," Ray said thoughtfully. "And you need this blade back."

"It is a matter of life or death for a whole lot of folks," Franklin said, repeating what he'd told Karl.

Ray might understand if it was ghost lives on the line, but Franklin still wasn't planning on mentioning it.

"Do you know who has the blade?" Ray asked.

"Dr. Traeger," Franklin said.

Ray nodded and took another sip of his beer. "He's a powerful man in this community. Lot of friends, particularly in law enforcement. He beat that lawsuit those patients' families brought against him."

"I know," Franklin said sourly. "We tried breaking into his house —me and Darryl—but we got caught."

"So you need someone with greater skills to steal this blade back for you?" Ray asked.

"Yes, sir. We do."

Ray was quiet for a moment, thinking. "I know somebody. They can get here by tomorrow," he said quietly. "But. Listen to me, Franklin. This is the first, last, and *only* time you ever ask me for this kind of favor. Whatever I may owe you or you owe me—this is it. Do you understand?"

"Yes, sir," Franklin said. Had he made Ray angry?

"Come by tomorrow at this same time," Ray instructed. He seemed so serious. It was a side of Ray that Franklin had never seen before—easygoing Ray replaced by someone a lot harder.

Had he ever shown this face of his to Adrianna?

They talked a little while longer, and Ray accepted a dinner invitation for a week later. But there was still this distance between them.

Franklin left sooner than he'd planned to, unsure of how to fix this.

He needed the help. He was certain, now, that whoever Ray brought in would be able to handle the job.

But how was Franklin gonna handle this new side of Ray?

FRANKLIN GOT BACK to the vegetable stand early. He didn't really have time to do anything else—if he biked to his farm, he'd only be there twenty minutes before he had to turn right around and come back.

Karl was sitting in the shade at the back of the stand, one of the high-powered fans blowing directly on him. He was reading some fat fantasy book—a habit he'd picked up since fighting the creature the year before.

Karl had always thought that the stuff made up in fantasy books wasn't true. Now that part of it might be, he told Franklin that he'd be doing his research to make sure he'd be up to speed the next time something otherworldly attacked him.

Franklin didn't bother telling him that most of what was in those books wasn't true, at least the ones he'd read about ghosts. And the made up words and languages just made his head hurt.

"You get your problem taken care of?" Karl asked as Franklin walked into the back of the stand, heading toward his popcorn making equipment.

Franklin looked over at Karl. He hadn't raised his head, and appeared to still be reading his book.

"I did," Franklin told him.

"Good," Karl said. "That's all I want to know. Don't want Sheriff Thompson accusing me of being some kind of accomplice or something."

"Wouldn't want that either," Franklin assured him. Sure, Karl had been instrumental in killing the creature the year before, and hadn't lied exactly about breaking Franklin out of jail, though he hadn't told the truth, either. Karl had just let Sheriff Thompson assume the worst.

A few moments passed while Franklin got out his popping corn and his big pan. Should he try for another fancy combination that day? Or just go for a straight forward mix?

"You think we might close up a little early Friday night?" Karl asked.

He was still sitting, still looking down at his book, not meeting Franklin's eye.

"We could," Franklin said. "Or I could just handle the stand on my own."

"Okay," Karl said.

When it appeared Karl wasn't gonna say nothing more, Franklin felt he had to ask. "Hot date?"

"You might say that," Karl replied, finally looking up, wearing a huge grin.

"I'm glad you finally asked the girl out," Franklin said. And he was.

What was it about being in love that made him want everyone else to be as happy as he was?

"How about you try a one-to-four combo this time?" Karl said, putting his book to the side and coming to stand next to Franklin.

"White to yellow?" Franklin asked. At Karl's nod, he continued. "Tried that. Too chewy. I was thinking of reversing it this time."

"But wouldn't that much yellow corn overwhelm anything you mixed in with it?" Karl asked.

"No, I don't think so," Franklin said, grinning.

And they was off, talking about their favorite subject, debating the right and wrong mixes and blends, getting into the fine details of a subject they both knew the most about.

Popping corn.

Because while Karl was Franklin's partner at the stand, he was still a competitor.

And maybe this year, Franklin would beat Karl and get that blue ribbon prize at the Kentucky state fair for the best-tasting popping corn.

CHAPTER 10

Franklin spent all Thursday night trying to figure out some other way of getting the blade away from Dr. Traeger, but he couldn't think of nothing. He weren't no superhero, able to run so quickly no one could see him. He couldn't leap over the walls around Dr. Traeger's house, or spin a web and fly on the strands.

Franklin's only ability was to help ghosts pass, and there weren't even any ghosts around. Since the year before, when he'd fought the creature, there had always been a few.

Was the doctor stealing all the souls who were dying in the area? Franklin wasn't sure where he'd put them, though. The blade was still full. Did the doctor have other containers that held souls? Like canning jars, that Franklin would keep in the root cellar beneath the house?

He could still feel the blade, impatient with waiting. It wasn't designed to *hold* souls, not long term, just take 'em and move 'em along.

Working at the fruit and vegetable stand the next morning was actually a relief, giving Franklin something better to do than to sit there and cogitate. After Karl left, Franklin spent his time perfecting a three-corn blend of popping corn, topped with rosemary butter. This corn he'd be willing to sell for a quarter.

Finally, it was time for Franklin to make his way back to Ray's house. The day had started out warm and just gotten hotter. Franklin pedaled slowly through the heat, still not sure he was doing the right thing.

All too soon he was standing outside Ray's gate. Before he pushed the pretty doorbell the door buzzed and swung open.

Franklin walked his bike into the yard and leaned it on the fence right close to the gate, even turning it around so he wouldn't have to later.

Not that he was thinking he'd have to make a fast escape or something.

The door to the house stood open, a dark hole cut into the gray stucco. Franklin walked forward slowly, pausing on the threshold. He didn't see no one. "Mr. Sorrel?" Franklin called. "Ray?"

What had happened to Ray? Had whoever Ray called turned on him, instead?

"Come on back to the office," came a mechanical-sounding voice right next to Franklin.

He jumped and turned.

There was a small speaker on the side of the door, like an intercom. Franklin had used those when he'd worked at the grocery store. He'd just never noticed it before.

"And close the door."

Franklin didn't want to close the door. He had a bad feeling about all of this. But he did as Ray asked, since that was his voice coming through the speaker.

The living room hadn't changed—Adrianna's art still crowded the bookshelves to the right, the extra chair still sat in the middle of what used to be open space, and boxes still sat all piled up next to the island of the kitchen.

Franklin got a better look at the boxes this time. They *were* moving boxes.

Bright sunlight poured through the big glass doors leading to the backyard. The hallway just beyond the kitchen was dark in comparison. More boxes sat along the left side, making it more narrow. It smelled of burnt toast and bacon, holding in the remains of breakfast, most likely.

Franklin hadn't been down the hallway into the rest of the house too often. But he knew where the office was. First door on his right after the kitchen.

Ray sat behind his desk, the only light in the room a fancy lamp, the light pointing down at the desk. The curtains behind Ray were drawn tightly shut, so no sunlight came in. Bookshelves loomed on every wall, the dark making the space seem tight. Two chairs stood on the other side of the desk.

Ray wasn't wearing one of his usual Hawaiian shirts. Instead, he wore a white shirt and a suit coat. His square jaw was clenched tight, and his eyes were harder than Franklin had ever seen them before.

"Good to see you, Franklin," Ray said softly. "Please, have a seat."

Franklin wanted to stay standing, but he did as Ray asked, choosing the chair on the right.

"I want to make sure I understand the *problem* you're having," Ray said, putting a strange emphasis on the word *problem*. "Dr. Traeger stole your knife. You'd like it back."

"I would," Franklin said. "It's important," he added.

Ray stared at him, looking like he was judging Franklin's soul.

Franklin was just about to stand up and tell Ray to forget about it when Ray nodded. "I'd like you to meet someone."

A shadow detached itself from the corner. Franklin would never have guessed there was someone else in the room with them. She came to stand next to Ray.

She wore dark clothes—Franklin would have guessed it was a jeans jacket over a black T-shirt. She wasn't black, but she wasn't white either, her skin the color of paper in old books that had browned. She wore her hair in tight braids racing over the top of her head, then dangling down with yellow and red beads on the end.

Dark freckles spread across her tiny nose. Her eyes looked like hard marbles, black and unforgiving. Her thin lips were pressed together hard in an uncompromising line.

When Ray stood up, Franklin got another surprise.

The woman barely came up to Ray's chest, and Ray was shorter than Franklin. She couldn't have been five feet tall, even.

Franklin stood as well.

"Franklin, I'd like for you to meet Odell," Ray said formally. "Odell will fetch your blade for you. I will cover her costs."

The woman Odell exchanged a look with Ray that Franklin couldn't read. Was that not what she'd agreed to? Was Franklin supposed to be paying for her services, whatever those were?

"Franklin and I have already worked out our costs and favors," Ray continued.

Franklin nodded warily when Ray turned to look at him. As Ray had said, this was the first, last, and only time they'd ever do something like this. Particularly since it brought out this hard side of Ray that Franklin had never seen before. It made him uneasy.

Ray asked, "Do you agree?"

Franklin hesitated for a moment before he nodded and said, "I agree."

He felt like he was agreeing to his doom.

"Now, you keep this phone on you. All the time. You take a shower, it goes with you in a baggie. You take a shit, it's in your hand. Got it?" Odell instructed Franklin.

Her accent was soft, and the words melodic. It placed her not as a local, but from somewhere close. Probably from someplace just south of Kentucky.

Where'd she and Ray meet? Had it been at one of the big picnics that Ray and Adrianna used to give?

The three of them stood in the kitchen with the shades drawn across the bright sunlight outdoors, mainly so no one could see in. Odell was paranoid about that.

"Yes, ma'am," Franklin said, accepting the phone meekly. He was relieved to see it weren't a smart phone, but a flip phone, like his own.

"I'll text you the address where to meet me to pick up the package," Odell said. "I expect you to haul ass to get there."

It took Franklin a moment to realize that by *package* she meant the blade.

"Got it," Franklin said. He paused, then added, "I don't got a car. But I'll ride my bike as fast as I can."

Odell opened her mouth then shut it again, and shot a mean look at Ray.

He merely shrugged back.

It appeared to be a draw.

"Now, Ray here says you can talk to ghosts," Odell said. Her voice grew a shade softer.

"Really?" Franklin asked, surprised. He'd never admitted to his ability to Ray before Adrianna had died, and he certainly hadn't talked about it afterward to him. Just seemed cruel.

Plus, Adrianna's ghost had never come to visit. He figured she went straight to Heaven.

"My Aunt Jamilla died a couple of weeks ago. Cancer," Odell said. "Think I could talk to her?"

"It don't work that way, ma'am," Franklin said firmly.

"Then how's it work?" Odell asked.

Franklin looked at Ray who shrugged.

It was Franklin's choice just how much he told her.

"I work with ghosts who's having troubles," Franklin told her. "I help 'em with what they need to let go of this earth, pass beyond."

Odell nodded at that. "And there's some ghosts involved with this blade? It's haunted?"

That sounded about right to Franklin, not without going into all kinds of details. "Yes, ma'am. It's holding a bunch of souls right now."

Every time Franklin thought about the blade, he felt the weight of it in his side. It weren't always pain, like now, it was just pressure, a cold silver weight pushing him down.

"I ain't worked with spirits before," Odell said, glancing at Ray.

"You can always back out," Ray said smoothly. "We'll find someone else."

"I didn't say that," Odell said. "I'm just saying it might be more complicated."

"We'll talk details after you finish the job," Ray told her firmly. "After."

Odell gave him a sly smile. "Just checking. You still got it, old man."

Ray barked a laugh. "Thanks." He paused, then added, "You need anything else from him?" He indicated Franklin with a nod of his head.

"Him being able to drive a car might be nice," Odell drawled. "But I got it." She fixed her hard look back on Franklin again. "You might want to think about stealing one."

Franklin just shrugged. He couldn't borrow any of his cousins' cars without explaining too much. And he really didn't want to bring Julie into any of this.

"By tomorrow morning, you should have the blade," Odell said.

"Good. Thank you," Franklin said.

Odell gave him a curt nod.

Franklin just hoped that he'd still be thankful by the time this was all over.

FRANKLIN WAS EXHAUSTED by the time he pedaled home, working alone at the fruit and vegetable stand after Karl had left early. It weren't some kind of holiday weekend, but that's what people were acting like, buying up everything they could.

Then Franklin had had to close down the stand and haul everything back to the fridges, lock them up tight. They'd never had any problems with vandals. Karl claimed it was because he came by sometimes at night with his shotgun, packed with rock salt, and just waited in the shadows.

He'd only ever had to use it twice, but word had gotten around.

Franklin had jumped just about out of his skin every time he heard a phone ring. But it had always been one of his customers, not the phone that sat heavy in his pocket.

Franklin was looking forward to a good long soak in his tub, though he'd keep the phone right next to him. He figured, knowing his luck, that Odell would call just after he'd fallen asleep.

But no, his luck weren't even that good.

Julie's car sat parked in his driveway, with Julie standing beside it, waiting for him.

Franklin weren't sure, but he probably would have been happier to see Odell, what with the glare Julie was giving him.

~

"Was you ever gonna tell me about being arrested?" Julie asked after they'd both gotten themselves a beer and had settled themselves out back, on the chairs there. The big bug zapper was tinging every few seconds, taking the mosquitoes out of the air that would have been eating Julie alive.

Franklin had never been that bothered with bugs—they just didn't seem to like the taste of him.

He sighed and considered Julie's question. He knew the right answer was to tell her that of course he would have told her.

But Franklin figured the truth would be better just then.

"I don't know," he said. "I didn't want you to be worried." He paused, then added, "And though you may not think it's right, I'm glad it was Darryl, and not you, with me. I didn't want you to get into trouble."

Julie nodded. "I know you was trying to protect me. But you got to tell me things. If I'm feeling like you're hiding and lying to me, we just won't work out."

"These things are dangerous," Franklin pointed out. "The ghosts. And the doctor. I'd never forgive myself if you got hurt."

"How do you think I feel? Knowing you're going into this danger alone?" Julie said.

"Still better than you getting hurt," Franklin said stubbornly.

"I can take care of myself," Julie replied. "Better'n you, sometimes."

Franklin opened his mouth then shut it again. There weren't no way to win this argument. And he hated fighting with Julie this way.

On the other hand, he knew he was right. He wouldn't put her into danger if he could at all help it.

After a long moment, Julie asked, "So how are you getting the blade back?"

"What do you mean?" Franklin asked. "I'm not trying to get the blade back."

"Franklin Kanly, I know you well enough to know when you're lying to me," Julie said. "And I also know you're too stubborn to just let that son of a bitch win. So how are you getting that blade back?"

"I can't tell you," Franklin said, knowing he was admitting to some kind of plan just by saying that much. They weren't married. Sheriff Thompson might threaten her job or something if she didn't testify against Franklin. And Franklin didn't want to put Odell at risk either. She'd come after him if he did.

That was maybe another reason why he and Julie should get married. So she couldn't testify against him. Though he didn't think he should mention that to Julie just now.

"What do you mean?" Julie asked.

She didn't sound mad. She sounded hurt.

"If you don't know, you can't be made an accessory, or something," Franklin explained. "But I'm gonna get that blade back."

Julie nodded. "So you don't say anything. Let me guess. You found someone to break into Dr. Traeger's place."

"I can't tell you that," Franklin said. It surprised him how much he really wanted to tell Julie everything.

"So, what, they'll meet you at a prearranged place?" Julie asked, her eyes narrowed.

Franklin felt uncomfortable under her gaze. Like she was trying to take him apart, following every twitch, every breath, as if she could see how hard his heart was pounding.

Telling himself to just relax like they did on those cop shows on TV wasn't helping a bit.

He licked his lips, surprised to see how salty they were from the sweat that had broken out across the top one. "No, ma'am," he replied. "Can you not ask me anything more?"

Julie reached out and took his hand, lacing their fingers together.

"It's okay. Someone's gonna call you, since you don't have a place arranged."

Franklin stiffened. He knew Julie was smart. He hadn't figured she was that smart.

"I can't·tell you," Franklin said softly.

But Julie was nodding. "I know I'm right. So I'm just gonna sit here and wait with you until that phone rings."

Franklin sighed. On the one hand, he really didn't want Julie to come with. He wanted to protect her, keep her safe.

On the other hand, even if she was blazing mad at him, it was still nice to have her here, by his side, in the quiet of the night, watching the stars come out.

JULIE WAS on her second beer while Franklin was still nursing his first when the phone in his pocket chirped.

"You gonna answer that?" Julie asked.

Franklin sighed and dug the phone out of his pocket. He hadn't been able to think of a way of ditching Julie all night. If he went out the back and into the fields, she'd just follow him. He couldn't get away from her on his bike. She had a car.

He'd considered stealing it, but knew she'd never forgive him.

And as much as he wanted to keep her safe, he wanted for them to still be a couple even more.

He flipped the phone open. The message said merely, "Averson's Fields."

Franklin paused, blinking. Odell had managed to sneak back up the lane without them hearing her? Of course she had. But why was she wanting to meet in the fields next to his house?

At least she didn't want to meet in his field. If there was to be a battle, at least his corn might survive that year.

He closed the phone and looked over at Julie.

"Don't you even think about leaving without me," she told him bluntly. "If you ride your bicycle out of here, I'll just follow you. And you can't really outrun me in my car."

Franklin bit his lip. "Okay. Odell—shoot, forget I said that name —is over in Mrs. Averson's fields. Waiting for me. You need to stay here, in the house. Where it'll be safer."

It wouldn't be safe. Dr. Traeger knew where he lived. So did Odell, apparently.

But he had to protect Julie, somehow.

Was this how Mama had felt all these years? Why she'd had to stay, even past death, until she was certain he'd be all right?

Did he want to be like Mama that way?

"I'll stay at the edge of the field," Julie told him. "But if I hear you call out or anything, I'm calling Sheriff Thompson. Then I'm coming in to get you."

Franklin would have preferred for Julie to stay away from the danger, but he couldn't lock her in the house, no matter how much he might want to. He had to let her come.

He weren't Mama. He knew Julie could take care of herself.

Though if Franklin got into some kind of trouble that Odell couldn't handle, well, Julie probably wouldn't be much good either.

Except as a nurse.

THE MOON WAS LESS than half-full when they stepped from the house, not adding much light to the driveway. Cicadas screamed in the fields surrounding them. The interstate seemed quiet that night, the trucks already gone home. No frogs added their belching tune, probably scared away by Odell, waiting for them in the field.

Franklin had a windbreak of tall linden trees to the south, between his property and the Aversons'. While they could push their way through the twisted trunks, it wouldn't be easy. So they walked up to the lane, then headed towards the neighbor's fields.

Mrs. Averson hadn't planted anything in the fields for years. But she did pay to have it regularly mowed. The wild grass grew past Franklin's knees, hearty and thick.

It was good soil, there. Just a shame she wouldn't lower her price, or let Franklin have those fields. He could grow some mighty fine popping corn.

Julie held onto his hand tightly. Franklin scanned the fields, looking for something out of the ordinary. As they approached the spot where Darryl said there'd been a parked car, a light suddenly appeared, far off across the field.

Franklin figured that was Odell, signaling where he should go.

When Franklin tried to let go of Julie's hand, to give her a last goodbye hug, she held on, not letting go.

Franklin just stopped. "What do you think you're doing?" he asked. "I thought you'd agreed to stay by the side of the road."

"I lied," Julie told him cheerfully.

Franklin stayed where he was, shaking his head. He didn't want to be having this argument here in the middle of the lane, but he would, if necessary. Odell would be angry, but this was more important. "You've been saying how could you trust me if I don't talk to you. Now I'm asking you, how can I trust you if you're gonna lie that way?"

It seemed to Franklin that Julie had thought she'd been being cute or something, but it just sat wrong with him. It weren't quite bullying, but almost.

Julie instantly stopped smiling. "I'm sorry," she said. "And you're right. I shouldn't do things like that if I want you to trust me."

"So you understand that you need to keep your promise, then," Franklin said seriously. "Else I won't be able to trust you." And while his whole heart ached at the thought of not having Julie in his life, he needed her to be true. Or else their relationship wouldn't be worth the effort.

Julie sighed and looked away. Franklin knew she was mad. But was she more angry at herself or the situation?

Finally, Julie nodded. "I'll stay here. But something goes wrong—"

"Y'all come riding in like the cavalry," Franklin said.

Julie suddenly let go of his hand and pulled him into a fierce hug. "You come back to me, Franklin Kanly. Or I...I don't know what I'll do. But you won't like it."

"Yes, ma'am," Franklin said, holding her back just as tight. "Don't want to lose you, either."

Julie surprised him with the kiss she gave him—soft and sweet, like the promise of spring. Then she let go, stepping back. "I got my phone right here. And 911 as well as the sheriff on speed dial."

"I'll only be a minute," Franklin promised her, knowing he was lying.

He didn't imagine Odell would cross Ray. But what if she'd been forced to make that call by the doctor? She did have an aunt who'd recently died.

Then he turned and started across the field, the tips of the grass wet with dew and soaking his jeans through at the knees. But he marched on, like a soldier, going to battle.

Fighting for those he loved, with only his love as a shield.

CHAPTER 11

TIME SEEMED TO STRETCH OUT, like wet leather, just waiting for that final snap, as Franklin marched across Mrs. Averson's fields. The pale moon above him gave off more light out here, unblocked by the trees. High, knife-thin clouds were stretched across the dark sky, hiding the few stars that were out.

The cicadas were deafening. Their cycling cry sent shivers up and down Franklin's spine. The smell of the good earth, though, under his sneakers, grounded Franklin. Reminded him why he was doing this, fighting for the natural way of things.

The light came from an old-fashioned kerosene lantern. Odell had flattened a large circle of weeds and grass, and stood at the edge of it, the lantern at her feet.

This was the first time Franklin had seen her stand voluntarily near a light. Her face was pinched tight, not giving anything away.

Was this a trap?

The doctor walked out of the shadows from behind Odell.

Shit. Yes. It was a trap.

He weren't in his scrubs this time, but wore a dark suit jacket, white dress shirt, and jeans. His hair was even more red now, and was starting to grow back. Despite how his face had fleshed out, he still had hard, beady eyes, like a weasel's.

"So, my worthy adversary, I see you have returned," Dr. Traeger said.

Why did the doctor talk that way? Was it because he was crazy? Or was it because he thought all of the future was gonna be looking back on this moment and judging his words?

"I almost feel sorry for you, for the path you've chosen," Dr. Traeger said. "But like the other fools who won't join me, you're just going to die."

With a flourish of his hand, Dr. Traeger reached into his suit and drew out the knife.

Suddenly, the pain in Franklin's side surged. The pulse of the knife under Franklin's skin beat harder, like a war drum.

The doctor paused for a moment with the blade before him, chanting an invocation in a language Franklin didn't want to learn, the sounds twisting his tongue. A sickly yellow glow bloomed around the doctor, like a cloud of plague surrounding him. Then he started waving the blade through the air, like a baton, as if he were conducting an invisible orchestra.

Ghosts sprang up between them, rapidly rising, like evil fog. The ghosts were already howling as they came into being, the noise as deafening as tornado winds.

Franklin couldn't just turn away and run. The ghosts would come after him. And all he'd be doing was leading them back across the field to Julie. So he stood his ground, grinding his teeth together, determined to stay and do what he could.

The doctor continued to wave the blade.

The ghosts surged forward.

Before Franklin could step back, they'd started passing *through* him.

The cold was so intense Franklin's teeth started chattering. His insides felt displaced, like someone had scooped them out with an ice cream scoop, then slopped them back inside him, nothing in the right place anymore.

"Stop it!" Franklin said. The ghosts were sapping his strength, making it hard for him to even shuffle his feet.

He still moved forward, closer to the doctor, more determined than ever to stop him.

The ghosts were all angry and howling, angrier, in fact, than usual.

They didn't want to go through him. They were being directed against what little will they had. It pissed them off more, made them colder and more frightening.

Franklin knew it was just a matter of time before he died, his heart frozen from fright and cold.

He had to stop the doctor. He caught Odell's eye, asking her, "Why?"

"Dude's gonna make me immortal," Odell explained. "Do you know what level of black belt I could get to with lifetimes to study? Wetwork ain't gonna be nothing compared to what I'll be able to do."

Her glittering eyes shifted from Franklin to the doctor, and she watched him intently. Greedily.

Franklin felt his own howl gathering in his throat. Didn't she understand? The price they'd have to pay for living so long was too high.

All of Franklin's future was being stripped from him. His life with Julie. The chance to grow old, gain wisdom with his aches.

No little girl to teach. No son to cherish. The natural cycle of birth, growth, and death, broken.

The noise both inside and outside of Franklin's head was deafening. The cold stabbed him worse than any knife. His sorrow multiplied.

Franklin couldn't hold it back any longer.

He threw his head back and howled.

The sound mingled with the winds, cycling up with the howls of the ghosts. It grew to an unnatural noise, born of desperation and fear.

Franklin continued to howl and pushed himself forward another few inches. He had to get to the doctor. Stop him, somehow.

The doctor paused in his conducting. His eyebrows shot up his broad forehead. He seemed surprised that Franklin was still there, able to move, able to defy him.

The yellow cloud faded and started falling off the doctor, peeling away like petals from a flower.

Was it Franklin's own howls that was doing that? Or had the doctor lost his concentration?

Odell sprang forward. She was moving so fast her hand blurred as she struck the doctor on his right shoulder—the hand holding the knife.

Franklin would have bet that normally, that kind of blow would have sent a body flying.

Doctor Traeger merely shrugged, taking a half step back.

Odell kicked the hand holding the knife, again, moving faster than Franklin would have thought possible.

Still, the doctor's arm didn't go flying up.

The knife, however, did.

Before the doctor could grab it, Odell had snatched the blade away.

Just as quick, she tossed it toward Franklin with an easy, underhand throw. "Do your thing," she instructed him.

Franklin normally wouldn't have been able to catch the blade. But it came straight to his hand, the haft smacking firmly against his palm.

It had, after all, always liked him better. It also felt to Franklin like the blade was relieved to be away from the doctor.

But now what did he do?

Doctor Traeger turned to Odell. "I would have made you immortal!" he snarled.

Odell just shrugged. "And then what? We'd a' killed each other off, one by one, 'til there weren't no one left. Always gotta have new recruits. Fool."

Franklin's surge of relief didn't last.

Now that he held the blade, the ghosts was turning to him. The blade throbbed in his hand, the power evident.

But the power of the ghosts was there too, the cold passing over him in waves.

Like the last time Franklin had held the blade in the face of ghosts, he felt a calm take over him, almost like a heavy curtain had been drawn between him and his emotions, his anger and his fear.

The blade moved Franklin's hand, bringing it up toward his face, like a knight giving a salute to his opponent.

One of the ghosts separated himself from the rest, a middle-aged white man. He wore a fancier jacket than the others, with brass buttons running in two lines down the front and embroidered patches on the tops of his shoulders. His face grew more distinct as he stood there, with a beard and mustache forming beneath his hollowed-out eyes.

Hell, Franklin would have sworn he kinda looked like Karl, or Karl's great-great-great-granddaddy.

The ghost held up his sword and gave the same salute back to Franklin.

Then he attacked.

Franklin had never been in a sword fight before—the closest he'd come had been attacking the creature the previous year, using corncobs as swords. He jumped back, swinging the blade wildly.

It caught the soldier's blade with a high-pitched *ting*.

The ghost pressed forward, fighting with finesse.

Franklin let the blade move his hand more, defending himself.

He couldn't back up none, though.

That ghost wasn't getting through him. Wasn't gonna be able to cross the field and go attack Julie, next.

That ghost needed to go back to where it came from. Pass back along into its well-deserved rest.

Franklin weren't no expert with a blade or fighting.

But he knew his duty. He'd been helping ghosts pass along most of his life.

The blade knew what to do, though.

Franklin stood tall and proud and started pushing back, directing his *will* and his *intent* at the ghost. Trying to use the blade, too, to send the ghost along. Back to where it came from.

The ghost still fought. He got in a good blow, the ghost's sword passing through Franklin's arm, the cold burning through his bones.

Franklin knew he couldn't survive too many blows like that. They was too chilling, likely to freeze his soul.

So Franklin pressed on. He wouldn't give up. Finally, he got a good solid hit on the ghost's chest.

The ghost stepped back, fading as it did, losing its shape as it turned to mist.

The next fancy-dressed ghost stepped up. He didn't need as much convincing, and weren't fighting as hard. He faded almost before Franklin finished his third pass with his blade.

The ghosts spreading across the field thinned out.

Franklin realized he was fighting the generals, and as they passed, they were taking their troops with them.

Still, some of the men fought desperate hard. They were still fighting the war. Even with the cold the ghosts generated, Franklin found he was sweating.

A solid hard noise made him look up.

Odell had flattened the doctor. She was sitting on his back. She grinned at Franklin and gave him a thumb's up.

Finally, only one ghost remained, steely-eyed and angry. He wasn't a general, but a regular enlisted man. The bandages around his head bled dark, glittering blood. His uniform had holes along the sides, through which the ghost's pale skin gleamed.

He didn't come forward to fight Franklin, though. He cackled madly, the sound sending chills down Franklin's spine.

Was this the solitary ghost he'd seen at the battleground earlier? The one who'd been with them in the trees for a while?

The ghost stalked over toward Doctor Traeger.

Odell leaped off her perch, getting out of the ghost's way.

Doctor Traeger rose unsteadily to his feet. He swayed…

…and the ghost seemed to catch him.

They embraced for a moment, a strange sight, the doctor living and breathing and in full color, the ghost white as early morning fog. They looked like long-lost brothers, holding on like they'd both just found each other after years of searching.

Then they passed through each other.

Except that on the one side, the body of the doctor fell.

And on the other, two ghosts now stood there.

The doctor started howling, a loud, startled sound that faded as he did, the other ghost grinning as he sucked the doctor's soul away with him.

Where had he come from? Was that strange ghost another man with power? A soldier who'd been killed, and just biding his time? That was all Franklin could think of.

The blade whimpered in his hand. He took a good look at it.

Before, the blade had had three ridges on it, forming a triangular blade. One had been shaved off, and the others looked soft, faded.

The blade wasn't an evil thing, no.

But it was wounded, and likely to strike out if Franklin just let it be. Or its power would draw another madman.

Franklin took the blade in both his hands and focused his will on *it*, now.

It was time for it, too, to pass along, to go rest.

The pain licked at Franklin's side, pulsing once more.

The blade itself didn't resist none. The souls that had made up the three parts of the knife unraveled, like a braid being untied, removing themselves from the cold metal. Winds sprang up across the field, rustling the grass. The smell of caves and wet, moldy earth filled Franklin's nose. Sticky spiderwebs passed across his hands, then faded and dropped to the ground.

Franklin pushed again. *Goodbye*, he said. *Thank you.*

The blade sighed to itself as it grew hollow, emptying itself into the air and the beyond.

For a moment, Franklin found himself somewhere else. It was a land filled with forests and meadows, the air tainted with violent colors. The smell of *prey* came from every direction.

It weren't his idea of heaven, that was for damned sure.

But the three souls that had made it up sure seemed happy to be there.

When Franklin saw the field again, he realized Julie had come marching across it. She stood next to him, her hand raised mid-air, as if she wanted to touch him but were afraid to do so.

Franklin wrapped a weary arm across her shoulders and pulled her in tight. The warm scent of her drifted up from her hair, soothing his soul.

When he looked up, he saw Odell squatting next to the doctor, her fingers lightly touching his neck.

"He's dead," she announced as she stood back up. "Died of a heart attack," she added firmly. "I'll make sure he's found safe and secure in his bed."

Franklin opened his mouth to volunteer to help, but knew it would probably be better if Odell did the work herself. He still tried to take a step forward, and faltered. He felt as empty as the blade he held.

Julie held him tightly as he leaned his weight against her.

"Now, what did I tell you about ending up back at the hospital?" she growled at him.

He gave her a weak smile. "Just need to rest up some." Her warmth seeped into him, all along his side, bringing him back to life.

"You sure you okay to take care of this?" Franklin still asked, catching Odell's eye.

"Course I can," she said. "You two disappear."

Franklin turned with Julie still helping, and started shuffling across the field.

"And Ray said to remind you, 'never again,'" Odell said.

Franklin paused, then nodded. He weren't ever gonna ask Ray for another favor, not even to pass his beer across the table. But he also knew he should have trusted Ray, that Ray would have found him a good person, a local, even, one who he could trust.

But he was still just as happy that Odell was only passing through, that she wouldn't be sticking around, that she'd be heading back south wherever it was that she lived. He weren't sure he'd ever trust her, not really.

As they walked across the grass, the night outside felt softer now, the air crisp and the wind chilly. Franklin shivered, realizing he still carried the blade.

"We'll have to give this a good resting place," he told Julie as they reached the lane.

"Tomorrow," Julie promised him. "Or the next day."

Or the next, or the next, or the next.

Franklin found himself grinning.

There would more days, many more days, after that as well.

THE CEREMONY for the blade's burial was small—just Julie and Franklin gathered together in Franklin's backyard.

Eddie had provided the box—plain pine, with the wood dyed red and the insides covered in a green felt so dark it were almost black.

The pain in Franklin's side had mostly gone away. He weren't sure if it would come back to haunt him, as it were, some nights when there were ghosts hanging around the property who'd gotten restless.

Franklin dug a hole right in front of his cornfield—the spot where that first ghost had entered it and passed beyond. He hoped that white man had found his peace, somehow.

They buried the knife that Sunday afternoon, Franklin slipping away from Aunt Jasmine and the rest of the family, claiming he still needed more healing time.

The day was clear and warm, the summer sun starting to make itself known. The pond in Mrs. Averson's field had already dried up, the frogs disappearing. Or had that been the ghosts? Wind blew the sound of the interstate over the pair of them, like the shushing of waves.

After Franklin put the box in the hole, he weren't sure what to say. "Rest in peace," he eventually came up with. "I wish peace for you and all those souls you've touched."

And good hunting, Franklin added silently, remembering that glimpse he'd gotten of that other world.

Julie added a prayer that she'd gotten from Eddie, asking Brigid and those other gods Franklin didn't believe in to help the blade find its peace. Then she took three of the four rocks she'd blessed with sage and rosemary and placed them on the wooden box in the hole. She gave the last one to Franklin, for him to place with the others.

Julie added, "Sleep and rest."

Then Franklin started filling the rest of the hole back in.

After Franklin finished, he and Julie stayed in the backyard, sharing a beer. The evening started to settle around them, the air still warm but growing soft.

Franklin knew that Julie had things to say. He weren't certain, but he thought he might have more words to share with her as well.

He still took his time, and gave her the space she needed to find her tongue.

Finally, she came out with it.

"Were you serious, earlier?" she asked.

Franklin merely raised his eyebrows at her. He weren't quite sure what time earlier she was talking about.

He certainly loved her, that much he knew.

"About starting a family," she finally clarified.

"Someday, yes," Franklin said.

She shot him a look. Was she anxious? Nervous?

Franklin reached across the white metal table that stood between them and took her hand. "Not now," he said, caressing the soft skin of the back of her hand with his rough fingers.

Julie seemed to relax. "I'm not ready yet, either." She paused, then looked out over the fields. "Maybe not ever."

Franklin paused. "I ain't gonna lie. I do want kids. More family." To be able to watch them grow up. To become the best dad he could be.

Maybe even pass along a little of what he'd learned.

But Julie seemed to accept that. Or maybe she was just happy he'd told her the truth. "What if they're like you?" Julie asked.

Franklin blinked, surprised. Was that what this was all about? Did Julie have problems with him and his ghosts? He thought she'd come to accept that part of him.

Though she didn't really know much about them, he had to admit. He'd always been uncomfortable talking about them with her.

"Then we'll raise our kids up right," he replied gently. "Train them to do their duty."

Julie sighed and took another sip of her beer. "I just don't know," she said softly. "Some days I think holding onto my own little girl would make the world perfect. Other days, well, maybe my world's already perfect enough."

"I can't make that decision for you," Franklin said. "And I'll try not to pressure you about it." They'd have a rich, full life without any young ones, he knew that.

Just as he knew that his heart would always ache sometimes for the little girls and boys he never got to hold.

Julie nodded. She appeared satisfied. "I'm not saying no to kids, not putting my foot down. I just don't know. However, if I do decide that I want kids someday, I'd like to have them with you," she said very softly.

Franklin tugged on their joined hands, pulling Julie into his lap. He kissed her softly, sweetly, giving her kisses full of promises and love. He didn't know what the future held for them. He'd just have to wait and see.

As things was starting to get interesting between them, Franklin's side twinged.

He stiffened.

"What's wrong?" Julie asked. "Am I too heavy?" she asked, starting to rise.

"No, it's not that," Franklin said.

He looked out past Julie.

A ghost stood next to the spot where they'd buried the blade. She looked forlorn, lost, though she was wearing what had probably been her Sunday best—a floral dress with a darker jacket, and pearls that still shone against her dark, black skin.

Franklin looked at Julie, then back at the ghost. Then he nodded, decision made.

He helped Julie stand up, then took her hand and walked the pair of them over to where the ghost was standing. He kissed her temple, then asked, "Trust me?"

She nodded slowly.

Franklin squeezed her hand one more time, then took another step forward.

"Good evening, ma'am," he said, addressing the ghost. "Fine night, tonight."

The ghost turned her look of longing toward him, then back out, over the field. Her *intent* flowed out from her in waves: She wanted to keep going, but she just didn't know how.

"I think I can help you with that," Franklin told the ghost.

Julie squeezed Franklin's hand, then walked back to where they'd been sitting, giving Franklin the space he needed to do his work, his duty.

It would take time, Franklin knew, for them to figure out all the ins and outs, between her work and his. Between time for them and time for his duty. And maybe family time, someday, as well.

But they could do it.

And maybe, just maybe, someday Franklin would get to have the only type of immortality he was willing to strive for…a little girl with Julie's smile and powers all her own.

ABOUT THE AUTHOR

Leah Cutter writes page-turning, wildly imaginative fiction in exotic locations, such as a magical New Orleans, the ancient Orient, Hungary, the Oregon coast, rural Kentucky, Seattle, Minneapolis, and many others.

She writes literary, fantasy, mystery, science fiction, and horror fiction. Her short fiction has been published in magazines like Alfred Hitchcock's Mystery Magazine and Talebones, anthologies like Fiction River, and on the web. Her long fiction has been published both by New York publishers as well as small presses.

Find Leah's books here.

Follow her blog at www.LeahCutter.com.

Come someplace new…
If you'd like to be notified of new releases, sign up for my newsletter.

I will never spam you or use your email for nefarious purposes. You can also unsubscribe at any time.

http://www.LeahCutter.com/newsletter/

Reviews

It's true. Reviews help me sell more books. If you've enjoyed this story, please consider leaving a review of it on your favorite site.

ABOUT BOOK VIEW CAFÉ

Book View Café is a professional authors' cooperative offering DRM-free ebooks in multiple formats to readers around the world. With authors in a variety of genres including mystery, romance, fantasy, and science fiction, Book View Café has something for everyone.

Book View Café is good for readers because you can enjoy high-quality DRM-free ebooks from your favorite authors at a reasonable price.

Book View Café is good for writers because 95% of the profit goes directly to the book's author.

Book View Café authors include Nebula, Hugo, and Philip K. Dick Award winners, Nebula, Hugo, World Fantasy, and Rita Award nominees, and *New York Times* bestsellers and notable book authors.

www.bookviewcafe.com